AHND

Sylas Seabrook

*For all those who grew up on the streets.
Don't let anything hold you back.*

Acknowledgments

This work, like every work, is made possible not through the efforts of one person but through the contributions of many.

Without my alpha readers, this book would not be what it is today. A special thanks goes to the alpha readers, Vanessa Day, Mel Friday, and Joesph Hand.

Adding finesse to the finished worked was the purview of my beta readers, and I'd like to thank Brooke Auckerman, J.C. Brice, Amber Gill, David Lee Hotaling, Madison Jacobs, Dahlia MacEachern, S.F. Rogers, and Juniper Wester for their valuable feedback.

While I've mentioned each of these remarkable people in a single line, they've provided so much to help *Ahnd* shine that I can't thank them enough.

Content Advisory

This book contains content not suitable for all ages. Sensitive topics include graphic violence and child abuse. If these topics are not for you, please select another work for your reading enjoyment.

Smiling

The sun warmed Ahnd's blanket, wrapping him in comfort. Unfortunately, it didn't stop the screaming, so he covered his ears and squeezed super tight, pushing his overgrown blond hair back.

"You think this is the end of it! I'll take everything you have, John. Gay? How could you do this to me?" Ahnd's mother screamed.

"*I'm* throwing you out, you drug addicted bitch. The only thing you'll be taking is your next high, just like you've been doing since before he was born."

The squeezing wasn't working. Sad, Ahnd crept out of bed and to his bedroom door, grabbing his blankie and pulling it up to his chin as he watched. It wasn't their first fight. They fought a lot, but this one sounded badder than the others. He was only eight, so he didn't understand it all, but he was pretty sure mommy was leaving.

His mother grabbed stuff from the coffee table—the things she had told Ahnd to never touch—and shoved it into her purse. She stopped long enough to sniff her nose. She did that a lot.

"Right. Make it all about me. This is about you and your guy. You want me out so you can get it on with him. You were never good in bed anyway."

His dad looked really mad when he slapped his mom. It made his beer splatter all over. She screamed and clawed back at him, scratching his arms, then he grabbed her by the hair and drug her screaming to the door.

"Get out, you bitch. Don't think of coming back."

Was his dad serious? She couldn't *think* of it? How would he know if she did? He was pretty mad. Maybe he had a way. Little tears pooled in Ahnd's eyes, and he put the blankie in his mouth, nursing on it out of fear. If he was thinking about it, which he was, then his home just changed a lot.

"Get your ass back to your room," his dad said, glaring at him.

Ahnd scurried into his room and crawled into his bed with eyes wide open, thinking about his mommy.

The door to the house slammed.

What was going to happen to mommy? What was going to happen to Ahnd?

That night, a new guy came to the house. He was friendly looking, but Ahnd was nervous. Did this guy know where his mommy was?

"Hi, Ahnd. I'm Alex, your dad's partner. We're going to be living together. Doesn't that sound fun?"

Ahnd turned and ran. No, it didn't sound fun. He had a mommy, and he wanted her. Why was a guy moving in? He had a picture in his head. It had mommy and daddy and Ahnd and smiles. It didn't have this guy.

But there were no real pictures of them smiling. There was always something bad happening. Ahnd wished hard that one day he'd have a picture of his family smiling. All the Mesixias together. Then everything would be okay again.

Thief

Ahnd screamed as he threw his headset across the room. It crashed against the wall and bounced, tumbling onto his bed. Glaring at the stupid device, he huffed and stormed out of his room.

"Ahnd, you need to manage your emotions effectively. You're nine. There's no reason for this behavior," his stepdad said.

Ahnd sneered at him behind his back and slammed the door on his way out.

"Ahnd," his stepdad yelled from the door. "Where are you going?"

"To play," he said, then hopped the back fence into the apartment complex behind them.

He was nine. Why did he have to report where he was going? And why to his stepdad? He didn't even like the guy. Ahnd grunted, then shrugged. What did he care? He folded his arms across his chest as he moped through the parking lot. He needed something to do. More than a dumb thing like his video game. Why did people always gang up on him? Didn't ever give him a chance to get good.

He circled around the parking lot and meandered down the street, passing a few shops on the right and abandoned buildings on the left. The park was just up ahead, and that's where everybody hung out. Coming up on the park's fenced in basketball court, Ahnd heard his name.

"Yo, Mesixia!"

Vestor was kind of scary. Made him pretty cool. He led Areth's pack, and Areth was definitely scary. That dude basically ran the underground, so Vestor was the right hand of the baddest guy around. And he was a teenager. And he was calling for Ahnd.

Ahnd dropped his arms and put on an indifferent look, strutting up to Vestor with a limp to his step. "Yeah? Sup?"

"Got something you're going to like. Check this out," he said, pulling out a video cam.

"What do I need that for? I got an Inves 100. I can record anything."

"Ah," he said, putting an arm around Ahnd's shoulder. "But look through the lens. It's like a whole new world."

He held out the video cam, and Ahnd lifted it up to his eye. It was clearer and more detailed. It was like the lens brought the world into focus. Vestor touched the camera and suddenly it was like the world was in 4D. He could move back and forth through a scene like a time traveler.

"There's more filters, too. Play with it," Vestor said, patting Ahnd's back.

"How much?" Ahnd asked, playing with the filters.

"Just a thousand coin. Easy money."

Ahnd didn't have a thousand coin and he couldn't get it. That was a lot of money. And he was holding that in his hands! He carefully handed the camera back to Vestor and said, "I don't got a thousand coin."

"Ah, such a shame. I knew you would like this, so I saved it just for you," he said, then sighed. "You know, Marve was able to get to his dad's Inves when he wasn't looking and get the money. I'm sure a good boy like you would never do that, but adults have so much money, I bet they wouldn't even notice."

That was stealing. Ahnd had never stolen anything. Stealing a *thousand* coin? That was a ton. Adults really wouldn't notice? It was such a nice camera. Maybe he could do that. Would his dad even notice?

"It's okay. I can see if Marve wants it. He knows how to get the money."

"Wait," Ahnd said, grabbing Vestor's wrist. "I'll do it. My dad comes back this weekend. Can I get it then?"

Vestor groaned, thinking about it. "I guess I can wait that long," he finally said. "But don't let me down."

"I won't!"

Ahnd eyed the camera again. It was a whole new world waiting for him less than a week away. He could wait, but he wanted the camera now. No way to convince Vestor to let him have it right now.

"Go have some fun. See you this weekend," Vestor said, patting Ahnd on the butt.

Ahnd ran off. He wanted to play basketball, but the teenagers wouldn't let him play, so he went to the wall ball game and joined in with some kids his age.

"I'm gonna get a video cam," he said to James.

"What kind?"

"A cool one. Even does 4D!"

"Nice. My parents wouldn't get me one of those. They cost a lot."

"Yeah. I know, right?" Ahnd said, smacking the ball. "My dad's getting it for me."

"Sweet. Your dad must have bank," James said with a sideswipe to the ball that sent Ahnd running.

"Yeah. Guess so," Ahnd said, catching the ball and returning it with a slap.

After playing for a few hours, Ahnd was tired and the sky was dark, so he went home. Alex, his stepdad, was sleeping and didn't wake as Ahnd snuck through the house to his room and crashed.

The next day, Ahnd was so nervous he thought he might throw up. He stayed in his room all day. He had promised to steal from his dad. Maybe he could just ask him for it? No, his dad would never say yes. He was always saying they were broke, though he never ran out of money for beer. Could he back out of the deal? He wanted the camera, but he wasn't sure if he could steal. Vestor never backed out of deals. How did he get himself into this?

He skipped meals and was starving and scared

when he went to sleep.

Ahnd woke to his name being called repeatedly. His groggy mind took a minute to process the voice. It wasn't that lame Alex, but...his dad! He hopped out of bed, almost tripping over his too-long PJs, and darted into the living room. "Daddy!" Ahnd said, running up to him and hugging his leg. "I missed you."

"I missed you too, little man. How's my boy?"

"I'm good. I've just been playing."

"Staying out of trouble?"

"No. But Alex is a goody-goody," he said, sneering back at Alex in his recliner.

"Oh, is he? I'll have to talk with him about that," his dad said, chuckling.

"Thank you. Boys gotta have fun, right?"

His father kneeled down and gave Ahnd a proper hug, then held Ahnd in front of him by the shoulders.

"You can have fun without getting in trouble. You need to listen to your daddy Alex. He's here to take care of you while I work."

Ahnd raised his lower lip, pouting, then bowed his head. "Okay, I guess."

"That's my boy. Now get some breakfast and get out there and play. Sitting around all day at home is not good for a boy your age. And I hear you've been spending too much time playing video games."

Ahnd curled his neck around like an accusatory snake and glared at Alex. Stupid stepdad. Ratting him out.

"None of that," his dad said with a pop to his

bottom. "Alex is helping to raise you good. Now, go eat."

Cereal. With sugar. Lots of sugar. That made breakfast good. Orange juice was yummy too.

"I hear you're not doing good in school," his dad said, popping open his first beer of the day.

"Reading is hard. I don't like it."

"I'm not asking you to be an academic. Last thing I want is for you to go to Alexandria. But I do expect you to meet minimums. When I come back next month, your grades will be better, right?"

"I guess so."

"I expect so."

"Yes, daddy," Ahnd said, afraid of what might happen if his grades weren't better.

As soon as he got to core, he was going to drop out. Anyone could drop out of core, but you couldn't drop out of basic. He only had a couple more years to go. Then those teachers and their stupid books with the messed-up words could go to Hell.

He finished his cereal, tossed his bowl and cup in the sink, then ran to his room and changed. As he jetted out of the house, he heard his father yelling about washing the dishes. Pfft. Pick an order. He'd already told him to go play.

Playing wasn't easy. How do you play when you're thinking about stealing a *thousand* coin? No, not thinking...gonna do. It's just too much to handle. Ahnd got hit by the ball a lot on the playground and he caught a look from Vestor. Vestor definitely wasn't going to forget, and Ahnd couldn't stop thinking about it.

Heading off the court, Ahnd stopped dead in his tracks as Vestor called out to him. "See you tomorrow, Ahnd."

Ahnd flipped his chin up at Vestor. "Yeah. Def."

He trudged home, then at the base of the stairs, lifted his head and tried to put on an honest-nothing-going-wrong-or-sly-here face and crept into the house. His dad was snoring and Alex was asleep on his recliner. This was the perfect time. It might be his only time.

Ahnd exhaled and walked softly, working his way around that one part of the floor that creaked. He took forever getting to his dad's bed. His dad's arm was hanging over the bed like he'd passed out from too much alcohol, still in his Inves 250. The room smelled like pee and warm beer. Ahnd curled his nose up and kneeled down to look at his dad's Inves wrist pad. The angle was a little off, but he could do this.

Touching the wrist pad like a feather, Ahnd navigated the menus and got to the transfer screen. He typed in 1000 and took a deep breath. He held the air in tight and swallowed, then pressed the button to transfer. A second later, his world changed; the confirmation dialog dinged. His father didn't even respond to the sound. He'd gotten away with it.

Ahnd looked out of the bedroom door, across the house to the hallway that led to his bedroom. All he had to do now was make his escape. He was already on his knees and didn't want to risk standing up, so he crawled on all fours to the bedroom door, then grabbed onto the doorframe to inch himself up.

Three steps into the dining room, Ahnd about pulled a daddy and peed himself.

"Dishes," his dad said groggily.

Ahnd had held his breath forever. He breathed out slowly, then took another breath and said,"Okay, daddy," as cheerfully as he could, then using every ounce of self-control he had, he calmly walked over to the kitchen where his cereal bowl and glass sat cockeyed in the sink.

Ahnd's heart slowed down as he washed the dishes, the sound waking Alex. "How's our little boy?" Alex said.

"Good. Had fun playing," he said.

Did they notice anything off in his voice? If so, they didn't act like it. He finished his dishes, then went to his room and flopped down on his bed. He didn't sleep. His mind ran like a racecar on an endless track of fear. He was going to get caught. He knew it. He couldn't take it anymore and snuck back out while the sun was still down.

The basketball court was like a huge jail that when he walked into it, he'd be convicted forever. He started going off in the other direction, but the money in his account was like a burning fire. He couldn't escape this. Not now. He turned around, put on his gimpy strut, serious face, and confident posture, then went to the courtyard. He checked his Inves. It was 2am. Vestor must not sleep because he was there cracking jokes with some teens.

"Got your money," Ahnd said.

"Ah, now that's my boy. I knew that camera was perfect for you. Boys, get the camera."

A teenager ran off, then Vestor gave Ahnd a flipped chin. "So, where's my money?"

Ahnd transferred the money, hesitating to see the huge number drop, and closed his eyes for the second it took to click the last button. His fate was sealed. Ahnd swallowed. "There you go."

"Nice," Vestor said, checking his wrist pad. "Pleasure doing business with you."

The teenager returned with the camera and Vestor signaled with his head to give it to Ahnd.

Magic was now his. He could see the world in a whole new set of dimensions and colors.

"Thanks," he mumbled, lifting the camera to his eye and turning away. Somehow, he suddenly felt relaxed. Now it was all worth it. The world was his to see any way he wanted.

Family

Ahnd strutted into his house thinking about all the wonderful videos and pictures he'd taken. Every type you could imagine. He'd looked up the camera, and the camera actually cost 10,000 coin. How Vestor got it to him for 1,000 was amazing. It was worth the 10k. He'd found the perfect place to hide it, too. No one would check there.

With a beer in one hand, his dad grabbed him by his Inves with the other and slammed him against a wall.

"You son of a bitch," he growled. "Where's my money?"

Ahnd screamed. "Let me go! I don't know."

His dad reached over and set the beer on the counter, face red as fire, then backhanded Ahnd so hard that it made his neck hurt.

"Don't lie to me. I know you took it. The transfer goes to your account."

Ahnd started crying. "I don't know. I didn't do it. Maybe you did it by accident?"

"Then send it back," his dad said with lethal simplicity.

"Okay, okay. Some boys threatened me. They said if I didn't do it, they'd beat me up. I'm sorry. I had to do it. I don't have the money."

"That was rent money, you bastard."

"John, calm down. You're hurting the boy," Alex said, but Ahnd's dad just shoved him back.

"Don't tell me how to handle my son. He's incorrigible. He only understands one thing."

He turned his vile temper back to Ahnd and sneered. "You're going to get every penny of that back, and you're not coming back in this house until you do," he said, then swung around, throwing Ahnd.

Ahnd's arms and legs flailed as he flew, knocking over the beer as he tumbled. He crashed into the door, busting it open, and tumbled onto the porch. He rolled into the street, hands first, collecting a road rash on his hands and face.

"Go, you punk," his dad said, kicking at the air. "I don't want to see your face unless you've got my money."

Crying, Ahnd pushed himself up and watched as his dad slammed the broken door shut, the door resting at an angle in the frame. Painfully, he dusted his hands off on his pants, then looked at his bloodied palms, his lower lip quivering with devastation.

Voices were loud; Alex was arguing with his dad. He wiped his face with the back of his hands and stood there for a while. He was nine. How could his daddy kick him out of the house? What was he going to do? He would have to eat. He could go without a shower for a while, but where would he sleep?

Hurting inside and out, Ahnd trudged to the only place he felt safe. It was 6am and the sun was bursting over the skyline. He wished he had his camera on him, but he could get that later. He needed help now.

He went to the courtyard, but it was empty. Apparently, Vestor did sleep. Ahnd had nobody and nothing except his camera, and that wasn't even on him. This was the worst day of his life. He huddled in a corner, knees folded up, and buried his face in his lap, crying until he fell asleep.

"What's Ahnd doing sleeping here?" Vestor said.

Still half asleep, Ahnd lifted his head, his hands stinging and crusty. "My daddy kicked me out. I can't go back without the money."

"I don't do refunds," Vestor said with a chuckle. "But you're a cool kid. I think we can make something of you. Want a family that doesn't turn its back on you?"

"Mhmm," Ahnd said, hopeful.

"Gonna have to prove you're worthy. Do you think you are?"

"Yes. I deserve a family," Ahnd said.

Vestor spun around, lifting his hands in the air. "Boys, we've got an initiate. Welcome him to the family."

Two teens peeled off from playing basketball, letting the ball bounce out of bounds and rebound off the fence. Their bodies swayed as they marched toward Ahnd, then leaned down and picked him up by his shoulders, pinning him to the fence.

"Don't fight it," one teenager whispered. "It happens to everyone."

Ahnd didn't know what they meant, but it quickly became obvious. Almost two dozen other boys lined up in front of him with sneers on their faces. This didn't seem like a welcoming family, and what was he not supposed to fight? A boy walked up to Ahnd and punched him in the stomach.

Ahnd screamed out, but the next boy decked him in the face. "Take it like a man," he said.

They came fast, punching him all over. Some stronger than others, all hurting. If he thought his father was a force to be reckoned with, this was a whole other thing. He cried and whimpered, but held back from screaming. His life felt like it was over. Were they going to kill him? How much of this could he take?

Finally, the teenagers holding him up relaxed their hands and let him come down. They helped him so that he would stand, then the boys lined up again. Would this never end?

"Hold your hand up," one of the teenagers whispered.

Ahnd didn't want to, but he didn't want to disobey either, so he slowly raised his hand. The boys all walked past him and gave him a high-five. He was getting his family welcome.

When they were done, Vestor walked up and

extended a plastic bottle of water. "Welcome to the family," he said, holding the bottle of water out for Ahnd. "You've proven you can take a beating. Now you have to show us you can get up."

Ahnd didn't know what that meant, but he was standing even though his legs felt like buckling. Did that count?

"Take a seat," the teenager said, then guided Ahnd to a bench.

Ahnd accepted the help, easing down onto the bench and taking a sip of water. As the water flowed down his throat, his body lit up with pain, probably from him moving, but everything hurt in every place right now.

"You did good," a boy about Ahnd's age said. "Tommy's the name. Tommy Und. We're bros now."

They exchanged fist bumps and Tommy sat down next to him.

"Do you got a home?" Ahnd asked.

"Yep. Right where my ass is," he said, patting his backside.

"What's wrong with parents?"

"Don't be worrying about others. You got you, and you got us. All you gotta think about."

"Yeah, I guess you're right," Ahnd said, reflecting as much as his tender body would let him think.

"Don't fight, huh?"

"No. Is that bad?"

"Yeah. Gonna be a street rat, gotta know how to stand your ground."

"Can you show me?"

"Get better. Andy'll show you. You're family now. We take care of our own."

Ahnd nodded, and Tommy left, so he laid back on the bench and just hurt. The sun rose in the sky and beamed down on him, covering him with another form of discomfort. He sighed. He might as well do something today that he liked.

Swinging his legs over the edge of the bench, he stood, feeling like an old, beat up guy, and weaved through the park. A few blocks down on the left, he slipped through a broken back door and navigated the halls of basic school until he got to his locker. He popped it open and for the first time today, smiled. Grabbing his camera, he put the world behind the lens and chose a filter to turn everything into anime—he was done with reality for today.

He wandered through the city streets, enjoying the animated scenery. He laughed as some arguing people took on their cartoon style, making them look sillier than ever. As he approached the park, he was amazed at the rendition of the trees. They looked magical as the filter tweaked vapor and gave it a second life.

Someone bumped into him, and he almost dropped his camera. The person bumping into him slipped his hand into the camera strap and jabbed the other hand into Ahnd's side. Ahnd almost doubled over from the intense pain and the camera slipped from his hands. The thief took off running.

"Hey! That's mine!" he screamed.

A whistle rang out from the courtyard into the forest, catching Ahnd's attention. It was Vestor. He was whistling with one hand and pointing with another. Teenagers were already running toward the thief.

The thief looked over his shoulder and stopped dead in his tracks. He lifted his hands up, camera in hand, then set the camera down and stepped back.

"I didn't know," he said.

The teenagers hopped over the camera and pounced on the thief. Fists flew as he cried out. The pile broke away, leaving the thief writhing on the ground. One of the teenagers picked up the camera and handed it to Ahnd.

"Here you go, bro," the teenager said.

"Thanks," Ahnd said, holding his side. He examined the camera and was relieved to see it was still okay.

Ahnd lifted the camera and returned to his world, this time setting the filter to allow the real world to come through a bit and placing the strap around his neck.

"Mesixia," someone yelled at him. "Catch."

Ahnd swung his camera around quickly, letting it fall free as he caught the package. It was a hotdog with mustard and ketchup.

"Thanks!"

He devoured the hotdog in three bites, chewing quickly and swallowing in gulps. Needing something to drink, he filled his water bottle at the fountain and took some sips.

After food, he went back to his camera world, changing through filters and mastering the universe through the eye of his camera. It wasn't much food, but it was something. It wasn't like home, but it was his new home. Life was rough; he needed to be tougher.

Street Rat

Ahnd's honeymoon was over the next day.

"Yo, Mesixia. Get your ass up."

"Who are you?" Ahnd said, not moving as he brandished a growling scowl.

"Andy, and when I talk, you move."

Ahnd scrambled and rolled his blankets up, then set them in the stack of blankets. They had slept in a big room in the basement of one of the abandoned warehouses. There was a strict policy on what to do and how to do it. It felt like the military.

"Good. Follow me," Andy said.

He took Ahnd out to the courtyard and ordered him to do some exercises. Jumping jacks, pushups, pullups, etc. Ahnd struggled, his muscles aching from yesterday's beating. Whatever he did wasn't good enough for Andy, but he kept trying.

"You did good," Andy said.

"Thought I sucked."

"You do, but you still did good. We'll keep going tomorrow."

Tomorrow turned into the next day, which just kept going. A week went by and all Ahnd did was exercise. When he wasn't exercising, he was behind his camera. Life was different now, and he was becoming different.

"Thought I was going to learn how to fight," he said.

"Twigs don't fight. You need strength."

"How long's that gonna take?"

"You think you're ready?"

"I don't know."

"Only one way to find out. Come here," Andy said, grabbing Ahnd by the shoulder and pushing him out to the wall ball area. "Protect your head," he added, demonstrating.

He started with light punches, swinging faster and hitting harder. By the end of the day, bruises covered Ahnd's arms. Ahnd knew there was more to fighting, but he was exhausted and hungry and didn't really want to push it further right now.

"Will I ever be as good as you?" Ahnd asked.

"I got a head start, squirt. Don't try to be better than me. You're not fighting me. Try to be better than the guy you're fighting."

Ahnd nodded and returned to his camera. Holding it with bruised arms was hard, but worth it. He loved his new world and felt like he understood Tommy's ass comment better. He wasn't homeless; he was just house-less.

The next day brought more exercise and more training. The next month brought more of both. That month turned into the next month, and Ahnd was feeling more confident.

"I think I got this," Ahnd said.

"You don't have shit," Vestor said from the side.

"What do you mean?"

"Fight me."

Vestor pushed up off his back and walked calmly toward Ahnd. "You beat me, then you're ready."

Ahnd's other brothers started snickering, and that was enough to tell him he was in over his head.

"It's okay. Still got shit to learn," he said, trying to sound tough while non-threatening.

"Hit me," Vestor said, standing two feet away from Ahnd.

Ahnd shook his head.

"I wasn't asking."

That sucked. That meant it was a command. Ahnd had no choice. If he was going to do it, he was going to do it right. He threw a fast punch directly at Vestor's jaw, but Vestor leaned back, grabbed Ahnd's arm, pulled him forward, raised his knee, and tripped Ahnd. As Ahnd fell, Vestor twisted his arm and forced him to land on his back, then put a foot to his neck.

"You're still just a street rat, kid. You can't defend yourself to save your life. Get up," he said, releasing Ahnd's arm.

Ahnd rushed to stand, then nodded. "Thanks," he said, grateful that he didn't get a beating.

"Any time," Vestor said, returning to the wall.

"What do I learn next?" Ahnd asked Andy.

"Gonna take you to the next level, squirt. Fighting ain't about playing fair. First it's dirty fighting, then some martial arts. You ready?"

"Probably not," Ahnd admitted.

Andy laughed. "Good answer. We'll start tomorrow."

"Ahnd," Vestor yelled as Ahnd headed to get his camera.

"Time for you to earn your keep," Vestor said as Ahnd approached.

"My keep?"

"You think food comes from nowhere? It's time you start bringing in more than you eat."

"Okay. Do we have money?"

Vestor laughed, patting one of the teenagers on the shoulder. "This kid's funny. You're going to steal it."

"Oh."

"It's not the first time. You stole from your dad, right? This is for food. We wouldn't have any if these uppities had their way. They'd just let us starve. Do you want to starve?"

"No."

"Then we have to take what we can get. Kids have been stealing to feed you. Only right of you to return the favor, right?"

"Yeah. I guess so."

"Show him how, Jeffers."

One of the teenagers stepped forward, rolling his eyes, and signaled with his head for Ahnd to follow.

"Don't let me down," Vestor said as Ahnd trailed the teen.

They walked a couple of miles down the street, took a left and went another mile. It was farther than Ahnd had ever been in the city. They stopped at a grocery store.

"Bigger they are, easier to rob," Jeffers said. "You're going to get caught. Fight and run. Just go in and act like you're shopping. Grab some candy bars, then *walk* out of the store. They'll try to stop you. Ignore them and keep *walking*. As soon as you get to the security gate, run as fast as you can. You have to get through before they trigger the gate."

"Why don't I just run to start off with?"

"If you walk first, they don't panic quick enough and you get closer to freedom."

"What happens if I get caught?"

Jeffers shrugged. "They call the cops and you get fined. Cops don't deal with kids. They figure it'll work its way up to the parents. Just don't say anything."

Ahnd nodded.

"Go. What are you waiting for?"

Ahnd entered the store and improvised. He grabbed a hand basket and went to the bread aisle, which was closest to the exit. He didn't grab any bread, but headed over and picked up a few candy bars, putting them in the basket. Then, he returned to the bread aisle to fake out security and make them think he was shopping. His last maneuver was to return to the stack of hand carts and set his in it, then he reached in and picked up the candy bars. He was right near the exit, so he just walked straight through it. No one even yelled at him.

"Not what I told you to do," Jeffers said. "But it worked. You're lucky."

His training went on for six months. Six months of pain and suffering and stealing. Six months of training eight hours a day and two hours of being a thief after. Six months of working out and getting in trouble with the law. Ahnd was stronger, faster, smarter, and unlike his brothers, he didn't have a rap sheet. He wasn't as cocky, either. He learned that it was better not to fight, if he could, but smarter to be ready to fight, if he had to. He was still a street rat, but he was becoming one to reckon with.

Mentor

"Mesixia, I got a job for you," Vestor said.

"Yeah," Ahnd said, coming over from the hand ball area. "What's up?"

Vestor lowered his voice and waved Ahnd closer. "Electronics. There's a new store. Need you to hit it."

"On it, boss."

A hit. That meant stealing what he could. He needed to shop by price tag and size. Keep it small so he could pack more. Keep it pricey so it made more money on the black market. The only challenge for this job was that it was a new store, so no one knew its security. It was his job to figure it out and report. Ahnd was nimble, so it made escaping easier.

His Inves, equipped with extra pockets, dinged. Ahnd checked the wrist pad. It was a message from Vestor with the location. Only three blocks away. That was a good sign; escape would be easy. First, he needed to stake out the place and see what kind of security he was facing.

"Back tomorrow," Ahnd said.

"That's my boy."

Ahnd killed the Inves holocall, then took the back alleys, appearing on the main street just across from the target, Pilston's Parts. He instinctively peeked in the trash and was pleasantly surprised to find a half-eaten hamburger and some leftover fries. Grabbing them, he sat down against the wall and munched down. He would look like any urchin, a dirty street rat with no hope and no future—part of the city background noise. He'd become used to that. Let people think what they wanted. He lived better than some of them, but not the uppities. They were the bane of existence, holding the people down so that no one could rise up. Pilston—he guessed that was the owner's last name—was probably not fancy enough to be an uppity, but he owned a shop, so he had to have lots of money. All store owners made insane profits off the backs of the workers. That's what made it okay to steal from them.

Around 6pm, Ahnd sat with hands on knees and watched as security lasers filled Pilston's windows. Cocking his head to the side for a different view, he saw another set in front of the counter. The owner walked out of the front of the store and locked it with a handprint, so that meant there was no back exit. The blonde owner was tall, definitely taller than Ahnd, and just strong enough to be able to hold Ahnd if Ahnd screwed up, but he was old. Like older than Ahnd's dad by a lot. He wouldn't be fast, for sure.

This was going to be a tricky job. He got up and

went to the back alley, huddling up against a warm wall, then dozed off. He had that half sleep down, the kind where you can get some decent rest, but no one can get the drop on you. The problem with half sleep is that it made the night feel long. He was glad when the sun peeked up.

Ahnd snuck back up the alleyway, but stopped a few feet from the front. He didn't want to be seen today. He pulled out a broken mirror shard from his pocket and positioned it to let him look in the store at the register, then waited.

At 8am, the owner showed up and opened shop, but Ahnd didn't move. He watched patiently. About every three hours, Pilston went to the back. Ahnd timed it. He had 135 seconds. He rounded that down to two minutes and set a timer. With any luck, the guy was peeing and that meant he wouldn't be able to respond. It was the perfect opportunity.

The clock struck 5:15pm with the afternoon sun lighting up the shop, shining straight across the window. It would blind Pilston and make Ahnd's job even easier. This job was getting easier by the second. As predicted, Pilston left the counter and went to the back. Ahnd triggered his timer and made his move.

He ran across the street, dodging traffic, and stopped abruptly at the door, opening it softly. A little buzzer sounded announcing his arrival.

"Be right there!" Pilston called from the back as Ahnd walked down the racks. He had enough time to make one pass through the store and exit. He checked his wrist pad. Time was rushing past. He moved down

the aisle, grabbing things with values in the hundreds
that could fit in his palm and dropping them in
pockets. Around the bend, near the front of the store,
he found stuff with values in the thousands. Of course,
he would keep them in sight of the counter. Ahnd
grabbed a couple of these, emptying one pocket to
substitute the more valuable prizes. The best prize in
the store was a gaming device that was up on the top
shelf. Ahnd stepped up on the bottom shelf to try to
reach it, then a hand swooped in and grabbed the box.

"Let me help you," Pilston said.

Ahnd ducked and rolled, trying to get past
Pilston, but the old man kicked Ahnd mid-roll and
Ahnd crashed into the counter.

"Not so fast, kid."

Ahnd's wrist pad vibrated. His time was up. No
shit. He stood up and raised his fists, but Pilston took a
step back.

"Never act like you're going to hit someone.
Either hit them or don't," Pilston said.

Ahnd didn't hesitate. He lunged forward and
swung an arm, but Pilston dodged, spinning around
and delivered a kick to Ahnd's back. Ahnd tumbled
forward, crashing into the wall but caught himself.

That gave him direct line of sight to the door.
He made a run for it, but Pilston said, "Uh uh," and
triggered the security bars. "You have something
that's mine. A few things."

Ahnd spun around, huffing, and snarled at
Pilston. "You want to fight, old man. Fine." He ran
forward, ready to pound the old man, but somehow

Pilston got the upper hand. The foot, actually. He kicked it from underneath Ahnd and Ahnd fell smack on his back. It winded him.

"The secret to winning a fight is not to start it, and if someone else starts it, not to get hit," Pilston said, then put his foot on Ahnd's neck. "Tell me why I should not call the authorities."

"Go ahead," Ahnd said, spitting to the side. "They won't do nothing."

"I see," Pilston said, lifting his chin high. "Then maybe I will."

He reached down and picked Ahnd up by the chest, then hung him on a hook on the wall. It latched solidly into his Inves suit and made wiggling useless.

"Let me go!"

"Let's see what we have here," Pilston said, emptying Ahnd's pockets. He put everything on the counter, then started banging away at his wrist pad. "That comes to 41,255 coin. Quite a haul. That will be what you owe me."

"They'll come for me, old man. Let me go now."

"Well, see, here's the thing. If I let you go, you'll try again, but if you disappear, then everyone will wonder what happened to the little boy sent to steal from the old man. They'll be more careful, maybe even choose a different target."

What did this guy mean? Disappear? Ahnd struggled, but there was nothing he could do. Even positioning his feet against the wall made him swing differently.

"You should learn when to struggle. That

device attached a web on the back of your Inves. It has a solid lock on you. You won't be going anywhere. It's not smart to rob a tech shop. Save your energy."

He started putting things away, ignoring Ahnd, but saying, "What to do with the little boy?"

"I've made up my mind. You have quite a debt to pay to me. I'll let you work it off, and in exchange, you'll learn to be a better man. Do we have a deal?"

"No. I don't need to be a better man. I'm nine and I can do whatever I want. Let me go!"

"Nine? And where are your parents?"

"None of your business."

"I'm trying to have a civil conversation. What if I let you go and you went back to your friends and they saw you had failed? How would they respond to that?"

Ahnd would be punished. Hard. Failure was for fools, and it was a bad idea to be a fool. He had failed, though. Either way, he was in for it.

"What do you want with me? Are you some perve? Like little boys? You're sick."

"I know an ancient martial art. One whose principle is that if you get struck, it is your fault. You should dodge and use the momentum of your dodge to strike your opponent. Did you wonder why you never hit me?"

"I don't care what you know."

"I will teach you. The price you pay is to learn. Everyone needs an education."

"I dropped out. Education is for Alexandrians."

"You have a street education. I can give you a

different type of education. Look, kid, there are a few times in your life where you'll have a choice. That choice can change your future forever. Most of the time, life does not give us choices, but forces us down a path of its choosing. Have you felt like that recently? Like you don't have a choice? Like your life is just running in circles and you don't get to choose the direction?"

Yes, he did. But he wasn't going to tell this guy that.

"You have a choice. Face your friends or find your future. What will it be?"

Why did adults always talk you to death? And what did he mean by find my future? Ahnd was getting a headache.

"What's in it for me?"

"Food that doesn't come from a garbage can, a bed, safety, an education fit for a good life, and a future of your making."

Ahnd bowed his head. "Fine," he said. "But screw me over and I'll screw you up."

"Deal. Now, if I let you down, are you going to run to your friends and be punished for failing?"

"No."

"Then I think I'll close for the day. We can go to your new home and get you cleaned up. First, what is your name?"

"Ahnd. Ahnd Mesixia."

"Nice to meet you, Ahnd. I'm Capo Pilston."

"That's a weird name. What are you captain of?"

"It doesn't mean captain, but to answer your question, my own life."

A New Life

Capo's house was simple, but amazing. He definitely had money, and he had a lot of tech. It was not in any major city like everyone else Ahnd had ever known. It was a white, flat house in the middle of a sprawling field of vibrant grass. Out back, there was a pavilion where he relaxed and practiced his martial art. To the side was a garden with all kinds of vegetables and a few fruits, like strawberries. It looked so simple, but it was also a fortress. A huge force field surrounded the perimeter of the house and he kept a cache of weapons, both vapor and electronic.

"If you run, there is nothing around for miles. You will starve or the wildlife will eat you," Capo said, concluding the tour of his house.

"So, I am a prisoner?"

"Of your own word. I can always take you back to Myeinth and put you back on the streets. Here or there? Which do you choose?"

"Here. You don't like vapor?"

"We'll come to that another day. Let's just say I

like freedom."

"Ahnd?" came a gentle woman's voice.

Ahnd jumped, not expecting another person. "Yeah."

"Ahnd, meet Dawn, my wife."

Ahnd relaxed and smiled. "Hi," he said with a wave. She was a looker if ever he saw one, and she had a platter with three plates on it. Food. He was starving. The last time he'd eaten was the day before.

They sat outside as the sun went down, eating deliciously seasoned vegetables on sticks with meat that wasn't fully gray all the way through, but melted in Ahnd's mouth like savory chunks of perfection. She served it with a spicy tea that enhanced the meal's flavor.

Capo lit fires in some metal bowls around the veranda and they sat there in the warm firelight.

"You were hungry," Dawn said.

Ahnd bobbed his head in agreement, wiping his mouth before speaking. "Staked out the place all day. Didn't get a chance to eat."

"I see," she said, clearly not understanding. Capo must not have told on him.

"Come. You must be tired," Capo said, leading Ahnd inside the house to an empty room. "You'll sleep here. This is your room now."

The room was small, with just a few decorations. Given the scratches on the wall, someone had used it before. Did he have kids here as guests a lot? It seemed kind of creepy, but he had a wife, so he must not be that creepy.

"Thank you," Ahnd said, then climbed onto the mat on the floor that served as a bed. It was more comfortable than the blanket on the floor he had been sleeping with.

Vestor would be mad about now, wondering where Ahnd was at. They'd have word out on the street that he'd gone missing. The longer he was gone, the harsher the punishment. He fell asleep worrying about what would happen when he returned to Myeinth.

His dreams startled him awake. He was sweating. Vestor had been leading a pack of kids chasing Ahnd through the streets and everywhere Ahnd turned, the pack appeared. They kept getting closer and closer until he finally woke up just before one of the kids grabbed his Inves.

"Did I wake you?" Capo asked, further surprising Ahnd.

"No. Nightmare."

"When our fears become our dreams, we must conquer our fears."

Whatever that meant. Ahnd got up and Capo pointed out the shower. He cleaned himself and they gave him an outfit that almost fit. It was a little tight around the chest.

"Where'd you get this?" Ahnd asked.

"Breakfast is ready," Capo answered. What was wrong with that question?

"What's the white thing?" Ahnd asked, staring at his plate. He recognized the sausage and pancakes, but not the white thing with a ball in the center.

"An egg," Dawn said. "We have fresh eggs. They don't have those in the city."

"Are you sure? They're supposed to be yellow and like a pancake."

"I'm sure. It's cooked over medium. Try it."

Ahnd cautiously poked at the egg. It split open and yellow sauce oozed out. He looked up, then back at his plate. What did he care? It was food. If they wanted to call it an egg, they could. Wasn't like eggs he'd ever seen.

He tasted it and it tasted egg-like, so he devoured it along with breakfast, which came with a different, more tannic tea this time.

"So, what do you do here?"

"Practice, read, meditate, and enjoy the scenery," Capo said. "Which would you like to do first?"

"Practice. I can't read. The letters are scrambled, and I don't know what meditating is, but I can't just sit and stare at the grass."

"Scrambled? I've heard words described like that before. He's dyslexic, dear," Dawn said. "We can unscramble the letters for you. Would you like that?"

Ahnd shrugged. "I guess."

"Practice, it is," Capo said. "Come."

Capo started with a basic stance, one that was a little different from what Ahnd knew. They practiced that for an hour, then it was on to basic moves. Ahnd knew most of those, so he learned quickly. The difference was that there was fluidity to the movements. Instead of blocking, you rolled with it in a way, then hit your opponent. They spent a few more hours practicing, but didn't get far. Ahnd was winded and needed a break.

"Now, it is time for some reading."

Ahnd sighed. Stupid reading.

They gave him books with different types of letters, but they were still jumbled. He could make out some words, but not entire sentences. It was frustrating.

"Try this one, Ahnd," Dawn said.

He grabbed the book and was amazed. The letters were in the right places. He started reading it aloud and got into the story. It was a fun one about a boy who went sailing around the world and discovered magical creatures.

"Well, that settles that," Dawn said.

"What?" Ahnd said.

"You're holding the book upside down. Your brain needs to see the letters differently than others. Now you know how to make the letters work. Try the last one I gave you, but turn it over."

Ahnd looked at the cover and turned the pictures upside down. The words in it unraveled too.

"Can I finish the first story? I like it."

"Yes, dear."

He scooted back on his bed against the wall and folded his knees up, continuing the story. He started to nod off but wanted to finish the next chapter, so he forced his eyes open and continued reading.

He woke in the middle of the next chapter, the book placed to the side of his bed. *Where did they get fun books for kids?* he wondered.

Meditation was like staring at plants, but even less interesting. Ahnd just didn't have the skills for that. Capo said it was his attention span, whatever that was. He didn't want to give meditation or staring at plants any attention.

The following weeks were filled with practice and reading. Ahnd convinced Capo to let him read instead of meditate and stare. That was a relief.

The weeks turned to a month, which turned to months.

"Ahnd," Capo said one day. "One day, you will leave this place. You'll return to the streets of Myeinth and to all of its dangers. I want you to be ready."

"Am I not doing good in my training?"

"You're doing great, but you need to learn more about weapons. First, I need you to understand something."

"Weapons? You're going to teach me weapons?"

"After I explain something to you. Do I have your attention?"

Ahnd nodded and stayed quiet.

"Great. I have taught you to dodge in order to strike your opponent, but you need to know more than that. The best way to win a fight is to avoid it, and violence is, as Isaac Asmiov said, 'the last refuge of the incompetent.'"

"What's 'refuge' mean?"

"It means that if you can find any way of handling a situation so that it doesn't involve violence, that way is better than those which use violence."

"Okay."

"I want you to promise me that you will only use violence as a last resort. I want you to promise me that you will try not to use violence unless you have to."

"I promise," Ahnd said, not fully sure why Capo was giving him this speech.

"Come with me," he said and led him to the weapons cache. "This lesson is so important that the passphrase is my reminder."

He took a deep breath, then said very seriously, "Violence is the last refuge of the incompetent."

The door to the weapons cache split from left to right, then each side squished, exposing a variety of very dangerous weapons.

"I'm going to teach you how to use each of these," he said, facing Ahnd. "The most important weapons to know are those which cause no harm. We'll start with those."

From Grops to Brumenites to Mæz to the Shield of Myeinth to Groptites, he covered everything. Weapons that drugged, disabled, disarmed, and even dealt death. Not all of them were legal, which was even cooler to Ahnd. He learned what they were and how to use them. It was so much for a nine-year-old to take in, but Ahnd ate it up.

Ahnd felt safe with Capo. He had a home here, but the time had come for a serious conversation. Lunch was fresh strawberries and meat sandwiches of some kind. The sandwiches had cheese and mustard on them, so they were perfect.

"Vestor woulda sent someone else after me," Ahnd said.

"Yes, he did. That boy was not as agreeable as you."

"Did you tell them where I was?"

"No, but they didn't have a chance to ask."

"He'll come after you harder."

"He did."

"What happened?"

"He found out what you found out. Some old men are not to be tinkered with."

"What's that mean?"

"It means he won't be coming back. People pick on people they can get away with picking on. I showed him there were easier targets than me."

That made sense. Ahnd was beginning to understand Capo better. The old man used a lot of philosophy, but if you got the words down, you could get what he was saying. Wasn't as easy as if he spoke plain English.

"I miss my dad. Stupid Alex, too. Do you think I'll ever be able to go home?"

Dawn looked sad for Ahnd, but he didn't want pity. He just wanted to go home.

"What's keeping you from going home, Ahnd?" Capo asked.

"I stole a thousand coin from him. He told me I couldn't come home unless I had it back."

"I see. That is a lot of money. I would say that money is not what's keeping you from going home."

"What is?"

"I'll show you soon. Ahnd, when is your birthday?"

"May 27th."

"That was a couple of months ago. You're ten now. How about we celebrate tomorrow?"

Ahnd's eyes bugged out. "Really? Yes! I'm ten now!"

Amused, Capo and Dawn laughed.

"Then we party tomorrow."

Homecoming

Ahnd woke to streamers in his room, trailing out and around the house. Excited, he rolled out of bed, leaped to his feet, and ran into the kitchen.

"Happy birthday," they called, then sounded off little horn trinkets.

"Thank you!" Ahnd said.

There weren't any presents, but there was a very pretty cake. It had frosting as green as Ahnd's eyes, with a one and a zero on top for his age, and little yellow flowers along the edges. Dawn had some cooking skills. The candles were lit, so he blew them out, closing his eyes and making his wish.

I wish this year is better than the last.

With a flourish, Capo produced a birthday card.

"For me?" Ahnd said, grabbing it and opening it.

"Happy birthday, Ahnd," the card began. "Your debt is now paid and you are free to go. For your birthday, we are giving you the thousand coin your father wants. May your path be filled with the beauty you have brought back to our lives." Both of them signed it.

"Are you freaking serious? A *thousand* coin? My debt is paid? I love you," Ahnd said, giving each of them a hug. "Thank you. Thank you. Thank you. I can go home again! When can we go?"

"Anytime you want. Do you want to go now?"

"Yes. No. I mean, I like it here. I like you. Will I see you again?"

"You know how to find me if you ever need to see me," Capo said. "Pack your things."

Ahnd gave Dawn another hug, then ran to his room and packed up the few things he had. He changed into his Inves and that's when it all became real. He was going to lose this and go back to what? Alex and his dad? Vestor and the gang? The mire that was Myeinth? He felt a little sad, but there was this huge part of him which felt he needed to be with family. Family matters. This was the right thing to do.

In the jet car on the way back—one of the few vapor devices Capo used—Ahnd stared at the window. He might never see this place again. See real trees and grass and...now he felt like he wanted to stare at them and meditate. It was too late. He was going back to his past, to his future, and leaving this place behind.

"Thank you," Ahnd said.

Capo nodded.

"You said you would tell me about vapor one day."

"I did," Capo said. "The world has an addiction to vapor. It needs it and it needs more of it. For thousands of years, we lived off the land and relied on our skills. Vapor has replaced our skills and dumbed down our world. It makes slaves of all of us. I prefer freedom."

That was more philosophy than Ahnd could wrap his head around, so he asked his next question. "Who was the kid?"

"The kid?"

"My room. Another kid was there before me."

"My son. The last I saw him, he was about your age."

"Where's he at now? Did he run away too?"

"No. He didn't run away, but I'd rather not talk about it. Is that okay with you?"

"Sure. Sorry."

"You're fine, Ahnd. Always keep your curiosity about life."

"I'm a pretty curious boy. That's for sure."

Capo chuckled, but Ahnd couldn't make out why, so he pulled a book out of his bag and started reading, falling asleep after a couple of chapters.

When the car slowed down, Ahnd woke and rubbed his eyes. "Are we there yet?"

"Almost. We're at my store. There's something we need from here first."

"We? Okay," Ahnd said, yawning, then laying his head back against the door.

"Ahnd, please wake up," Capo said, turning to him.

"Huh? Okay. Is something wrong?"

"Books are very hard to get. You can't take

them with you."

"Awe. That sucks."

"I have something else for you, but first hand me all the books."

Ahnd reached in and pulled out his four favorite books. He hadn't taken them all. Frowning, he handed them over to Capo. "I didn't even like reading before."

"I know. Come with me."

They went into the store and Capo grabbed a visisheet. The device was two thin bars that pulled apart, revealing a stretchable, interactive screen.

"This is the best model I have. It should last you a long time. Be sure to take care of it. Here, you can read all the books you ever want. Let me disable the auto-rotate so that you can turn it and make the words easy to read."

"Oh, man. That's so sweet. Thanks, Capo. You're the best. I'll take real good care of it."

"I'm sure you will," he said, patting Ahnd on the back and handing him the visisheet. "Now, let's go to your home."

The problem with home is that it moved. The person answering the door had no idea who Ahnd was or where the previous tenant had gone, but Capo located him by name. Fortunately, there weren't many John Mesixias. The address took them deeper into the slums. Ahnd didn't care. He'd finally be home, and home was where his ass was. Tommy had taught him that.

Ahnd knocked on the door. It was a weekend, so his dad should be home. Alex answered.

"Ahnd! It's so good to see you. I've been worried sick about you. John, Ahnd is here!" he said, leaning down and offering a hug, but Ahnd hesitated.

"Where is that son of a..." his dad said as he came around the corner, stopping mid-sentence as he saw Capo. "Who the hell are you?" he added, using his beer bottle to point at Capo.

"I'm a friend of your son's. He said he lived here, so I brought him home."

Ahnd's dad reached out and jerked Ahnd in by his Inves, then slammed the door on Capo.

"You cost me my house, you bastard!" his dad yelled, then backhanded Ahnd.

Ahnd yelped, and the door flew open.

Ahnd's dad flipped his head to look at the door and growled. Capo stood in the opening as calmly as ever.

"Tell me you didn't just hit your son," Capo said.

Ahnd's dad curled his nose up and busted his bottle against the wall, brandishing it at Capo. "Get the hell out of my house."

Capo leaped into the house, performing a low overhead kick, and swiped his foot through the beer bottle wielding wrist. Ahnd's dad cursed, then raised his fist, but Capo swung his foot up from a standing position, placing it against Ahnd's dad's neck and pinning him against the wall. He leaned in, doing the splits standing—it blew Ahnd's mind away to see—and got in Ahnd's dad's face.

"I lost my son when he was eight. I would give

anything in the world for another minute with him. If I ever so much as get a hint that you've touched Ahnd again, I'll be back, and you won't like it. Blink if you understand."

Ahnd's dad couldn't breathe the way Capo had him by the neck. He blinked, then Capo lowered his foot, putting it straight down on the ground without even losing his balance.

"Ahnd," Capo said, kneeling while Ahnd's dad grabbed his neck and swore, then stormed out of the entryway.

Ahnd ran up to Capo and gave him a hug. "You have my contact. If you ever need help, don't hesitate to call. A victim is only a victim if they can't or don't defend themselves. Don't let it be the latter."

Ahnd wasn't sure what a ladder had to do with it, but he nodded. He was pretty sure Capo meant to defend yourself from everyone, even if it was your daddy.

"Sir, you can't just break into someone's house and attack them," Alex said.

Capo raised up off his knees and looked Alex directly in the eyes. "You seem like a reasonable man. Try to act like it."

"Take care, Ahnd," he added, then Capo vanished through the door, slowly pulling it closed as much as it would go, having just been kicked in.

Slinking, Ahnd went to his father's room. His father was pacing back and forth, rubbing his neck, and swearing. "I have your money, daddy."

"About damn time. I need more beer. Send it to

me, then get out of my face. I don't want to see you until my neck feels better."

Ahnd was lucky. The new house had a room for him. His daddy had been waiting for him. That gave him some comfort, even if his dad wasn't comforting. His old bed was there too, but nothing else. That was okay. He had his visisheet now, so a world that captured his imagination was at his fingertips. He jumped up on his bed, scooted back in the corner, and held the visisheet open.

Leader Of The Pack

Ahnd woke with his head leaning against the wall corner, slobber leaking out of his mouth, and his visisheet snapped up in front of him. He'd fallen asleep reading again. He scooted off the bed, tucked his visisheet under the mattress, then grabbed a cereal bar from a cupboard. It was night, but breakfast was always good.

He had a little money left, so he took a transport across town. When he'd left, he'd left his camera behind. Now that he was back, his first order of business was to get it back. This wasn't going to be easy, but the camera was his and like Capo said, "Don't be a victim."

He was dropped off near the school, so he made his way to the park, strutting across the park with the confidence of a teenager. He was spotted almost immediately. Vestor was pointing in his direction, saying something Ahnd couldn't hear. The other kids circled around, surrounding him as he approached.

Ahnd walked right up to Vestor.

"I'm here for my camera," Ahnd said.

Vestor laughed. "Thinks he can just disappear and come back making demands. Kid grew a set. Where have you been?"

"Got a mentor. Took me away. Not actually sure where I was, but I'm back. Don't live here anymore."

"You're part of the family. Once in the family, always in the family. You owe me for those lost electronics."

"Don't got it. Job was a fail."

"Well, when you fail, you know the price. One way or another, you've got to pay."

"Don't do this, Vestor. I'm not the little boy you knew."

Vestor chuckled. "He's not a little boy anymore. Boys, teach him a lesson."

Four teenagers stepped forward.

"Just take your beating. It'll be over soon," the boy leading the group of teenagers said.

Ahnd swept a foot back and calmly raised his hands to block his face. The teens charged. Ahnd lifted his foot, kicking one solidly in the nose, then leaned down on his hands as he thrust a foot around and swept the feet from under another. One got ahold of his Inves and jerked. Ahnd rolled with it, tumbling into a somersault, then pushed himself up into a standing position and kicked the kid straight in the nuts. He crumpled as the last teenager marched in, punching his hand like he planned on punching Ahnd's face. Ahnd was in his base stance and waited. The teenager got close enough and Ahnd leaped forward. As the kid raised his hands to defend himself, Ahnd kicked and hit home in the kid's neck. The kid dropped like a withered stream of vapor.

Ahnd made a run for it, charging directly at Vestor. Vestor whipped a gun out and it began charging, but Ahnd leaped to his left and spun with his body turned sideways to match the ground, kicking the weapon out of Vestor's hands and landing on his hands and feet. He spun around and knocked Vestor down, then jumped up and landed on his chest, his foot on Vestor's neck. He pressed down on Vestor's neck and looked at the teenager to his left. "I asked for my camera. I'm not going to ask again."

"Get it," Vestor wheezed.

Ahnd held his position until the camera was in his hands, then walked off of Vestor. Vestor scrambled back up, picking up his gun. Ahnd was ready for him. He activated an extension to his Inves from Capo and kept walking.

"Don't you turn your back on me," Vestor said, then shot. The bullet hit the Ementhium shield around him and ricocheted off. "Damn you, Ahnd! Don't you ever come back. You're done with this family. Done!"

Ahnd had his camera. He had his books. He had his freedom. He had his confidence. And he had his family, even if it was a mess.

Lifting the camera up as he exited the park, Ahnd began streaming the world through the eyes of his lens. He felt comfortable again. He wandered through the streets, back toward the transit stop, and hopped on, taking him back home.

The view with the 4D filter of the transit moving along the streets was amazing, almost dizzying. It ended all too soon for Ahnd. He wasn't ready to go home, so he meandered through the city, taking in the sights through his camera. There was something about capturing the world around him that felt empowering.

The streets were enticing. He liked the feeling of being in a street family. Wherever you went in the city, the streets were owned, and if you followed the tree up far enough, it was to the same top dog: Areth Kivinston. You rarely saw him; he stayed way below the radar, but he was a legend in his own right.

Ahnd dropped by his house and secured his camera under his bed, then it was back to the streets hunting for the pack leader in this part of the city. He found some street rats and approached them.

"Looking to join. Need a family," Ahnd said.

"Talk to Larry," a particularly ragged street rat said.

"Where's he at?"

"Warehouse on Tvari and Main," the ragged street rat answered.

"Thanks, bro."

"Ain't your bro yet," he said with a sneer.

Ahnd flipped his chin up at the kids, then headed to Tvari and Main. The building had one door that was cracked open. He slipped inside and immediately drew attention.

"Don't got nothing on me," Ahnd said, raising

his hands.

"What do you want?" Larry, their leader, said.

"Outta Vestor's pack. Need a new one."

"What makes you think we need you?" Larry replied.

"Can fight."

"Prove it," Larry said, waving a few teenagers forward.

Ahnd got into stance and waited for them to approach. They charged and Ahnd laid them out, then walked over one and stopped in front of Larry. "I'm in?"

"Yeah. You're in," Larry said.

Birthday Boy

Two years later, Ahnd was rising in the gang. He'd established himself as a strong member of the family with a wicked set of skills. But Ahnd's twelfth birthday sucked. He didn't even go home. He rarely went home anymore. Home was where his ass was, and that was rarely in his dad's place.

His family, his true family, his street family, threw a bit of a party. It involved some gunshots, alcohol, and girls that made Ahnd feel uncomfortable. They threw in a cake freshly stolen from a bakery, too.

That was the good part of his birthday.

After the celebration, Ahnd was more than a little tipsy. He sat down on a bench, trying not to feel sick, and a girl sat next to him, putting her hand on his leg and rubbing it. He bit his lower lip and swallowed, lowering his head and seeing her chest. He took a deep breath and squirmed while some of the other boys laughed at him.

"Let's have some fun," Larry announced,

flipping a couple of knives in his hand and catching them.

"Gerald and Tom, you're up," he said, holding the knives with their handles out.

Two teens jumped up from the benches, leaving their girls behind, and sauntered over to Larry, taking a knife.

"Have to stay in the circle. First one to draw blood wins."

They entered the center circle of the basketball court, each on one side of the midcourt line, then began dancing on their feet, the blade extended. Tommy lunged forward, slashing to the left at Gerald's right hand, but Gerald hopped back, almost going outside the circle. Gerald took the chance and leaped forward, coming down at an angle. Tommy didn't dodge fast enough and the blade cut his Inves at the shoulder. Tommy slapped his shoulder, then looked at his hand and held it up. It had blood on it.

"Gerald wins," Larry announced.

Another few pairs went up to battle while Ginny, the girl touching Ahnd, kept going higher on Ahnd's leg. He grew so nervous at her touch that he could barely focus on the fight.

"Birthday boy Ahnd and Rusty, you're up," Larry called, much to Ahnd's relief.

Ahnd jumped up and grabbed a knife, then entered the center circle. Rusty was taller than Ahnd, which should give Ahnd an advantage. Ahnd was also really fast. Usually. He was drunk, so a little slower today.

Ahnd started by bouncing from foot to foot, but then got it together enough to go into his fighting stance. He'd learned how to fight with a knife, so he kept his hands low like the other boys. Rusty didn't play games and had no mercy. He thrust forward and Ahnd dodged...but he screwed up and dodged the wrong direction. The knife pierced his stomach and a pain like no other sliced through his body. Ahnd checked the wound, then stared in shock at Rusty as Rusty withdrew the blade. Ahnd couldn't feel the blade slip out of his body, but he could feel that something was wrong. Rusty had hit something important.

Ahnd collapsed to his knees, his legs refusing to work—from the wound or the shock, he wasn't sure—and tumbled forward.

"Grab him," Larry said.

Ahnd felt a few teenagers' strong arms lift him up, his feet dragging on the ground. Someone must have spawned a car with a Mæssan device, a device that created physical vehicles directly from Mæssium vapor. Ahnd was shoved into the car. He wasn't thinking clearly and his eyes weren't registering what was around him. All he knew was pain, throbbing, intense pain. It was so much he couldn't even cry.

The car stopped and they dragged him out, then he heard the car zooming away. They left him. Left him to die on the side of the street.

"We've got a stab victim," someone said. "Get the gurney!"

Ahnd was lifted up, then it was all just too much

for him and he faded out. When his eyes opened, he was in a hospital room. He tried to get up, but he wasn't going anywhere anytime soon. He groaned and reached for his side. That was tender, so he flopped back on his bed.

"I see someone is awake," a woman said. "We have some questions for you. Let's start with your name."

"Ahnd Mesixia."

"How old are you, Ahnd?"

"Twelve."

"Do you know where your family is?"

Ahnd shrugged and instantly regretted it. His body didn't want him to move. "No," he said, breathing hard. "Try dad. Never home."

"What's his name?"

"John Mesixia."

"Okay. That's all for now. Your spleen was punctured. We had to remove it. You also had an excess of fluid in the brain. You'll be able to go home in a day or two, but you will have to limit physical activity for four to six weeks. The doctor will tell you more."

They found Alex, probably through Ahnd's dad. The last person Ahnd wanted to see was super sappy Alex. He came rushing into the room.

"Ahnd, Ahnd. I'm so glad you're going to be okay. Tell me what happened. Who did this to you?"

Ahnd turned his head to the side, ignoring Alex.

"Come on, Ahnd. I'm always here for you. Don't push me out. But if you don't want to talk, you don't have to. I won't force you."

"Wanna go home," Ahnd said.

"They're releasing you tomorrow, but I brought this," Alex said.

Ahnd turned his head to the side. His stepdad had gone digging through his room and found his visisheet.

"I thought you would want it."

"Stay out my room," Ahnd said, slowly extending a hand out to take the visisheet.

Alex handed Ahnd the device, then took a seat. "I'm staying here with you tonight. I want to make sure you're safe."

"Doing Fine. Go home."

"This isn't a choice, Ahnd."

Ahnd wanted to shrug, but remembered the pain, so he just slowly extended the visisheet and pulled up his current book. He turned the device so that he could see the words, then started reading.

"Ahnd, I need to tell you something," Alex said. "I noticed it already. There was a fluid buildup in your brain. It looks like it affects your speech. You'll be okay, but know that I'm here for you if you need to talk about it."

Ahnd grunted. His brain? His speech? He was never going to be the same again? How was that okay? He clenched his jaw, fighting back the urge to cry, but it screwed up his reading. He couldn't focus. How did a jab to the stomach mess with your brain? Was he really going to be okay? It was too much to think about, so he sighed and let the thoughts swim through his head until he fell asleep.

The next day, Alex hauled him home. His father wasn't there, which was not a surprise, and Alex fawned over him like he was a hurt puppy. It was annoying, but Ahnd didn't really want to move anyway, so he begrudgingly accepted the care. He had to put up with it for almost a month, but he gained strength and everyday it got easier to get out of bed to go to the bathroom.

Finally, he felt like he could make it on his own. Alex was smothering, so Ahnd waited until night and Alex was asleep, then snuck out of the house. He made it to the warehouse, strutting in and resisting the residual pain.

"Ahnd!" Larry said. "You made it! Nice. Lost the fight, though."

"Wanna learn. Teach me fight with weapons street style," Ahnd said.

"Getting a little big there, eh?"

"Street don't care. Why me?"

"Good attitude. What's up with your speech?"

"Side effect. Don't matter."

Capo had taught him how to fight with and against opponents with weapons, but the next few months educated Ahnd in ways he never thought possible. He got some cuts and other wounds, but he made it, and he was that much more lethal. He even pulled up some books on fighting with weapons and studied those. He didn't want to lose another fight like that, and did everything he could to make sure he would come out on top. Don't be a victim. Capo had taught him that.

Rules

Ahnd held up his camera, taking in the world through his new filter. He'd built this filter to make everything into a wireframe colored by the distance from him. It was almost like he could see through buildings, even though he knew he couldn't. It let him see people within the buildings when he overlaid a heatmap on top of the filter.

Life at thirteen was pretty sweet. He had a girl, a solid position in the street fam, a place to crash, everything he wanted, and he was a teenager. What else was there? The world was out there, and he could do whatever he wanted.

"It's going down tonight," Tommy said.

Tommy was a good friend. After Ahnd had taken on Vestor, Tommy had followed him to the other side of town. He'd proven reliable; he had your back if you had his.

"Dumb fight, ask me."

"Is what it is. Can't go talking about a guy's girl. You wouldn't let someone talk about Vera."

That was true, but people knew better than to
mess with Ahnd. Mesixia would lay you out faster
than a bullet to the brain—he helped you fall faster.

"Spot?"

"Yeah. Abandoned building on 3rd and Toreen."

Ahnd looked at his wrist pad. There were still
three hours before the fight. This fight had Ahnd
worried. Most fights broke out and ended in seconds
with bruises and cuts. This was a duel with hot
emotions involved. Something about it put him on
edge. He shrugged. Wasn't his fight. No vapor in that
game.

Ahnd let his camera fall to his side, grabbed the
Mæssan he lifted off some mark, and Mæssaned a
hoverboard. "Coming?" Ahnd asked, and Tommy
tossed out his Mæssan, spawning a hoverboard.

They leaned back on their boards and the
vapor vehicles shot forward. Hopping back and forth
across the street, they weaved their way through the
city toward 3rd street, then took a sharp left and
skated to Toreen. There was already a group of people
assembling. They vaporized their boards and flipped a
chin to the door guard as they entered.

A pile of sand was in the center of the building.
A red Mæssium vapor line surrounded the circle with
a two-foot buffer and a solid blue strip of Ementhium
vapor cut the circle in half. The surrounding zone was
for the referee, and the dividing line was for the start
of each round. Up to three rounds. If no one drew
blood after three minutes, then it went to another
round. If after three rounds, there was no winner,

then it was a draw. Only blades were allowed, no guns or vapor.

Around the circle, the two gangs assembled, taking sides while they talked, laughed, and cajoled each other. Each side had about two dozen members assembled, and there were still two hours to go before the match started. Ahnd grabbed a bottle of water from a metal bucket filled with ice and popped the lid.

"Ahnd," Larry called.

Ahnd flipped his chin up at Larry and swaggered over to him.

"Yeah. Sup, boss?"

"Placing a bet? I got two-to-one on Juge in round one."

Juge was Larry's guy. Ahnd had occasionally sparred with him. He was good, but slow. Ahnd doubted he would win in round one. His opponent was called K and came from Vestor's group. K was younger by a year and faster, but he lacked Juge's skill. If anyone were going to win in round one, it would be K, but Larry knew how to dodge. He'd work K down a bit, then strike.

"Taking same in two," Ahnd replied.

"Two-to-one on Juge in round two? I'll take that. He wins in round one, you lose."

Ahnd nodded. "Two-fifty."

"Two hundred and fifty coin it is."

Ahnd wandered into the crowd, saying hi to his buddies, his family, but there was something in the air tonight that bothered him. It took him some time to put a fix on it, then he knew exactly what was wrong.

The other side was too quiet.

"Ain't right," Ahnd said, approaching Tommy. "Vestor's peeps quiet."

"What do you make of it?"

"Something going down. Not what it seems."

"Yeah. Better let Larry know."

"You?"

"Sure. I'll let him know. Gotta keep our eyes open."

Ahnd grunted, and Tommy fell back into the crowd. Ahnd skipped out a back door and Mæssaned a car, then hopped in and zoomed down the street. He called Capo on the car, and his hologram appeared.

"Ahnd. It's good to see you. It's been a long time."

"Need you. Big fight. Weapons. Lotta guys gonna die."

"I see. Hold on."

Capo disappeared from the hologram for a second, then came back.

"I've programmed the code of zero-five-two-seven-seven-two-five-zero into my store. Do you got that?"

"Yeah."

"Call me when you get there."

Ten minutes later, Ahnd screeched to a halt in front of Pilston's Parts and jumped out of the car, leaving it spawned. He lifted his wrist pad and called Capo back as he entered the store.

"In."

"Go to the back on the left side of the counter,

then face to your right."

Ahnd obeyed.

"There."

"Say my favorite quote.'"

Ahnd repeated the quote about violence and the wall split in two horizontally, then each half compressed like a window blind exposing a weapons cache.

"Do you see the Groptite?"

"Yeah," Ahnd said, grabbing the purple sphere.

It was a smart little weapon, activated by pressing the buttons on the top and bottom at the same time. He dropped it in a side pocket.

"Thanks, Capo. Gonna save lives."

"Anytime, Ahnd. You're a good man. I'm proud of you."

The wall sealed up, and Ahnd left, locking the door behind him. He raced back to the match.

De-spawning the car, he entered the building and acted like nothing happened, but Tommy caught him.

"Where'd you go?"

Ahnd shrugged. Tommy took the hint and stood silently next to Ahnd as they watched the crowd.

Twenty minutes later, KJ stepped into the center of the ring.

"Let's get this show on the road," he said. "Larry, Vestor, send out your referee choices."

Vestor called out three names at the same time Larry did. Ahnd was in Larry's list. He grunted, then took his place on one side of the sand. KJ set a bottle down in the middle and spun it around. It twirled, then came to a stop dead center on Ahnd.

Ahnd groaned.

"Ahnd is the referee. Blades only, no going for the eyes or cock, no vapor, and the match ends when first blood is drawn. If you strike again, you lose. Does everyone understand the rules?"

The room echoed as everyone shouted, "Yes!"

Ahnd stepped into the ring around the sand, and KJ called the contestants forward.

K and Juge took opposite sides of the blue Ementhium line, each taking the side where their gang was grouped and looking lethally serious, though K looked a little too sure of himself.

"Shouldn't have talked shit about my girl," K said.

Juge grunted, then flipped a knife in his hand. K pulled two knives out of his pockets, one in each hand, and grinned toothily.

"This is going to be fast," K said.

Ahnd stepped into the sand, raised his hand, pressed a button on his Inves to start the timer, then swept his hand down. "Three minutes," he said, stepping back.

K slashed forward, going for Juge's wrist, trying to take out his knife hand, but Juge swung his hand out and K missed. Juge took the chance to flip his hand around and stab forward, but K jerked his arm and hit Juge's forearm, causing his knife to miss K's torso.

They danced like that for the duration of the

round, neither getting an advantage and neither cutting the other.

Ahnd's Inves vibrated.

"End round," Ahnd yelled, stepping into the circle with his hands spread. "Take sides."

The two opponents returned to their sides, K huffing more than Juge. Juge was tiring him out, slowing him down. Ahnd was going to win the bet, but he still didn't feel right about it. Both sides cheered their fighter on, and Ahnd gave them two minutes.

"Positions," Ahnd said.

They took up their fighting stances, but this time K reached behind him and pulled another longer blade, throwing his smaller blade into the ground.

"Going to cut your ass, Juge. You're mine."

Ahnd started the round and the timer, then stepped back. K immediately lunged forward, but Juge somersaulted under him, grabbed the knife in the ground, and stopped in a crouch. He spun around and drove the knife into the back of K's calf.

K screamed and turned around as Ahnd stepped in to call the fight. The moment then turned into a movie going frame by frame through Ahnd's lens on the world. K reached around with his right hand and pulled another weapon from his back. It shined against the barrel fires inside the building, and Ahnd's instinct took over.

Ahnd jumped up into the air, kicking just as K took aim at Juge. His foot hit home and the gun spun out of K's hand. Still in the air, Ahnd reached up and grabbed the gun. He landed on the ground, twisting his ankle. As he crashed down to his knee, his hand tightened and the gun went off. Ahnd froze.

K's knees collapsed down to Ahnd's level, then he fell over backwards. Ahnd looked to his right and saw the most gruesome sight he'd ever seen. The bullet had sheared K's face, leaving a bloodied mess. Ahnd blinked, filled with shock, and dropped the gun.

"Violence is the last refuge of the incompetent." Ahnd was a fool, a murderer. What was he going to do? This was worse than he could possibly have imagined.

He closed his eyes, holding back tears, then decided there was only one thing he could do. Own it.

He stood up and said, "No cheating." He headed toward Larry's gang, but the slow-motion movie hadn't ended. Both sides pulled guns. Ahnd reached in his pocket and pressed the buttons on the purple sphere.

Purple Groppenium vapor exploded in a massive sphere around Ahnd, coasting through everyone as a second, orange sphere of Tituerium vapor rocketed out of the device in Ahnd's pocket. The wave of Groppenium locked everyone in place, turning them into living statues, unable to control their muscles while the Tituerium zapped the vapor from every weapon.

Ahnd was the only one who could move, but everyone could hear.

"Break the rules, pay the price. Ain't gonna fight," Ahnd said, piercing the silence of the room like a commander.

Stoic, Ahnd sighed, looking at K again. The last still frame of this movie cut into his mind like a carving in stone. Leaving, he Mæssaned a car and zoomed off.

Price Of Peace

K's face was plastered across the windshield. Ahnd looked left and his face was on that window. Down and he was on the dashboard. Everywhere he looked, K's mutilated face followed him as if it were emblazoned across pupils. K was following Ahnd, and Ahnd couldn't escape.

Ahnd hit the brakes and screeched to a halt, then ran from the car, darting forward, panicking, with tears streaming down his face. He had to get this out of his head. He was a killer haunted by his victim. K deserved it, didn't he? Who deserved that? No, he couldn't. No one did.

Ahnd tripped, falling into someone who cursed and kicked at him to get off them. He climbed to his feet and kept running. Where was he running to? He wasn't running to anywhere; he was running from K. And he couldn't escape.

He grabbed his head and squeezed tight, trying to wring the vision from his head. He shook his head back and forth and spun around, falling into a wall, then sliding down. He buried his head in his knees and screamed. What was he going to do? He banged his head against his knees.

"Get out!" he cried. "Just get out!"

Ahnd grew numb to life, numb to the visions, numb. He started shaking. He was breaking down. It was consuming him. Ahnd needed to get a grip. He started measuring his breath, opened his eyes, looked up at the people passing by. He could do this. He was Ahnd Mesixia. He exhaled slowly and wiped the tears from his face, then took a deep breath and blew it out.

"Got this," he said, encouraging himself.

Ahnd drew his hands over his head, looked up at the sky, then stood. He breathed in and out again, then Mæssaned a new car. He didn't know where he was going, but he had an urge to keep moving. He took to the highway and drove. Endlessly forward.

K didn't go away. His face, his taunts, his jabs replayed over and over. It was like his peripheral vision was plagued with a permanent memory. Ahnd needed help. He called Capo.

"Twice in one day and you're crying. How can I help, Ahnd?"

"Killed him. Shot him. In my head. Won't leave. Help," Ahnd said, his voice cracking. "Please help."

"I'm on my way. Go to the shop and wait for me."

Ahnd nodded, then took the next exit and sped to Pilston's Parts. He sat in the car, head on the steering wheel, watching the movie torture him, punish him, thrash him repeatedly.

A rap came at the window.

"What?" Ahnd said without looking up.

"Come inside, Ahnd," Capo said.

Face red with agony, Ahnd climbed out of the car and slunk into the shop. Capo came back with a cup of tea and handed it to Ahnd.

"Tell me what happened."

"Bro pulled gun. Kicked it. Caught it. Twisted ankle. Gun shot. Took his face. Blood everywhere. Can't get it out. Ghost trying kill me."

Ahnd took a sip of the tea. It was relaxing, calming, so he took another sip.

"I think I get it. Why aren't you speaking in full sentences?"

"Brain got hurt. Got stabbed," Ahnd said, pointing to his Inves where the stab wound was hidden.

"I'm sorry, Ahnd."

Ahnd took another sip of his tea. "Help me?" he begged.

"I am."

What did he mean? What kind of help was he giving? He was just asking questions. Ahnd swayed. The tea. There was something in the tea. He glanced at Capo as he fell to the side. How could Capo drug him?

Ahnd blinked, wincing at the bright light. He hadn't slept long. He felt exhausted, drained. Where was he? There was a wall. He recognized it. He was back at Capo's house.

He crawled out of bed and went to the back

porch. Capo was there, drinking tea.

"Poison?"

"Not exactly. I sedated you. The mind needs time to heal."

"Can't heal this."

"True. You will live with it your entire life, but you can learn to live with it."

"Can't live with death."

"I have something I want you to read."

It wasn't some*thing*, it was a library. And it wasn't stories; it was people's thoughts and sayings. Philosophy. People thought about all kinds of things and they thought about death a lot, but none of them had murdered someone else. What was the point of all this reading? It was interesting. Ahnd enjoyed it. He liked this better than reading other people's stories. It made him think about who he was and what made other people tick.

But it didn't take away his ghost.

"Not finding nothing," Ahnd told Capo.

"Then you're not asking the right question. What are you looking for?"

"Need him leave."

"That's a tough one. If I were you, I would try Koram's *Reflectiod*."

Capo spelled that out. It wasn't in his library, so Ahnd looked it up using a visisheet. It was old and the language was difficult, so he had the app rewrite it into simpler English. Koram had thought about everything, even the dark. He put himself in the shoes of people who had done it all. You could see how they felt and feel for them. It was creepy and cool. Ahnd found his section. Someone going through his situation. Someone facing his ever-present demon.

I WALKED THE STREETS OF ORINTH, A MAN'S BLOOD ON MY HANDS, HIS DEATH IN MY HEAD. HE LIVED THOUGH HE WAS DEAD; HE LIVED IN MY MIND. AN APPARITION AFFLICTING MY SOUL, HE CREPT THROUGH MY CONSCIOUSNESS. I WANTED TO TEAR AT MY SKIN AND RIP HIM OUT OF MY BODY, PEEL HIS MEMORY FROM MY FLESH. I THOUGHT I WOULD GO INSANE. WAS I ALREADY THERE?

HE WAS AN AGONIZING PLAGUE I COULD NOT ESCAPE, A CONQUERED FOE WHO WOULD NOT YIELD, A POISON RAVAGING MY CONSCIENCE. I BECAME HIS VICTIM, NOT THE VICTOR. WOULD THIS NEVER END?

FORGIVENESS COMES FROM MY VICTIM; MY VICTIM COULD NEVER FORGIVE. ABSOLUTION COMES FROM RESOLUTION; MY SUFFERING IS WITHOUT END.

SEASONS ROLLED BY AND MY EYES GREW POOR, BUT HIM I STILL SAW. MY EARS BECAME WEAK, BUT HIM I STILL HEARD. MY MIND DULLED, BUT HIM I STILL KNEW TO THE END.

I TOOK A MAN'S LIFE; MINE HE CLAIMED IN TURN.

I LEARNED ALONG THE WAY NOT TO FIGHT MY FATE, JUST LIKE THE MAN COULD NOT FIGHT HIS. I LEARNED ALONG THE WAY TO CARRY MY BURDEN, AS HE COULD NOT CARRY IT FOR ME. I LEARNED ALONG THE WAY TO BE A BETTER MAN, FOR I FEARED THE MAN WOULD GET A FRIEND.

Ahnd had taken a boy's life, and he would be forever haunted by the boy's ghost. There was no escape, no break, no hope. All he could do was be better than he was and make sure it didn't happen again. Ahnd cried. He was sorry for what he had done. Now he would have to face it and carry that burden his entire life. Koram was right, and Ahnd didn't want to give K a friend. He didn't know if he could handle it.

Silently, he took another couple of days to think about what Koram had written. Really, he was accepting it. And if he didn't accept it and move on, walk with his sin and accept his punishment, then K would have killed Ahnd too.

"Ready go home," Ahnd said on the third day.

"You found your answer?"

"No. Found truth."

"I see. Sometimes they are not the same thing. I'm sorry, Ahnd. I wish I could do more for you."

Ahnd flipped his chin up at Capo. "Saved lives. Groptite bomb good."

"I'm glad to hear that."

Capo dropped Ahnd off at his dad's house. "Anytime you need me, just call."

Ahnd flipped his chin up, and Capo took off.

Rep

"Mesixia," Larry called as he leaned against the building where his gang congregated while Ahnd approached. "Where you been?"

"Chasing ghost."

"Big stunt you pulled. Thought you chickened out and ran."

"Don't run."

"Good. See, that little stunt you pulled caused me trouble. After the bomb wore off, all hell broke loose. Got a lot of boys hurt."

"Killed?"

"Nah, but you're going to make it up to them."

Ahnd positioned himself in his fighting stance, ready for the onslaught.

Larry laughed. "We're not going to fight you. I have something else in mind."

Ahnd relaxed, standing upright. "What's that?"

"Where'd you get that bomb?"

"Friend."

"Well, your friend is going to give you a lot

more weapons. I'm betting where that came from, there's a ton. Am I right?"

"No."

"Ah, now, Ahnd, don't lie to me. I know there's more there."

"Not lying. Telling no."

Larry kicked himself off the wall and sauntered up to Ahnd. He got in Ahnd's face and said, "No one tells me no."

"Just did," Ahnd said, not moving a muscle.

Larry started to raise his fist, but Ahnd struck first. Hard and fast, straight to the sternum. He felt the bone crack under his force and watched as Larry flew back and smacked his head hard against the ground. He was gasping for air. A couple of teens ran over to him.

"Needs doc," Ahnd said. He turned around, spreading his hands wide, and yelled, "Ahnd Mesixia don't take orders."

Ahnd went over to Tommy and flipped his chin up.

"Got a set," Tommy said.

Ahnd shrugged.

"Not gonna be able to stay in the gang, you know?"

Ahnd shrugged.

"Friends?" Ahnd said.

"Yeah, bro."

Ahnd nodded, then gave Tommy a fist bump and went home. Hopping on his bed and scooting back against the wall, he pulled out his visisheet and started reading, but he chose different books—books on philosophy. They were more interesting.

Ahnd had lost his girl—she was with the gang—had lost his street family, didn't have a real family, but he had a place to crash, a ghost with him to help keep him in check, thoughts of really smart guys to keep him company, and food to eat. For Ahnd, that was good enough.

"Mesixia," a boy called as Ahnd made his way home.

Ahnd turned around, keeping his head high, then groaned. It was the enforcer, Taddias. Word spread fast when you took out a gang leader.

Ahnd assumed his fighting stance.

"They said you would try to fight. You realize how stupid that is, right? No one beats me."

Ahnd held position.

Taddias sighed and charged for Ahnd. Approaching, Taddias pulled something out of his pocket and swung it at Ahnd. Ahnd reached up to block, but it exploded into bolts of electricity. Great, a Mæz. He didn't even have time to think as the electricity coursed through his body and brought him to the ground.

Taddias came up and kicked Ahnd in the side as the electric shock subsided.

"This is going to hurt," he said.

Ahnd groaned and rolled to his right side, sneaking his right arm into a side pocket of his Inves. He took another kick directly to the spine, then rolled back over, the knife held up behind his forearm where

Taddias couldn't see.

"No one takes out a gang leader. You've done two. Punishment is severe," Taddias said, pulling his foot back and aiming for Ahnd's face.

As his foot came forward, Ahnd reached up with his right hand and pushed the foot up. It sailed over his head, and Ahnd continued pushing until he leaped forward into a handstand while Taddias lost his balance and righted himself.

Taddias immediately took advantage of Ahnd in a handstand, coming into kick him straight in the nuts, but Ahnd brought one leg down on Taddias' foot while he swiped the other across Taddias' face.

Taddias stumbled, ending up on his knees while Ahnd went with the rotation of his body and righted himself into a standing position.

"Missed it," Ahnd said.

"What?" Taddias said, lunging forward with a powered up kick-punch duo.

Ahnd dodged, spinning around while he flipped out his knife from behind his forearm, then kneeled down at the same time that he faced Taddias, driving the knife straight into his upper thigh.

Taddias screamed and Ahnd took a step back, then kicked forward, clipping Taddias by the jaw. Taddias flopped backward with such force that his skull hit the pavement and cracked.

"Knife," Ahnd said.

Ahnd sighed, then went home.

"Ahnd, what did you do?" Alex asked, poking his unwanted head into Ahnd's room.

Ahnd raised a brow.

"There are some huge guys here to see you. They're rather pushy."

At the door, the guys stepped aside and extended an arm. "The boss wants the pleasure of your company," one of them said sarcastically.

The arm pointed towards a fancy car. In the car, the big guys didn't say anything. It stopped and they got out at a nightclub called the Lucky Lady. Ahnd was escorted to a room on the second floor. Inside, it was as rich as the car and a guy in a suit that cost a fortune sat in one of two plush chairs.

"Ahnd, I take it?"

Ahnd flipped his chin up at him.

"I'm Areth Kivinston. Please have a seat."

That wasn't really a request. He was the biggest drug dealer on the planet and head of Groppen One, the corporation centered in none other than Alexandria itself, the place where anyone who went in never came out. Ahnd felt like he should be nervous, but he hadn't come alone—K was always with him and he was much scarier. Ahnd took the seat.

"You're an interesting kid, Mr. Mesixia," Areth began. "You have a home, but prefer the streets. You've been in two gangs and beat up two gang leaders and my enforcer while managing to keep a clean rap sheet. Every now and then you disappear for a while and no one can track you. You haven't completed core, have access to illegal weapons, and there was the unfortunate incident at the fight.

"As you can tell, I've had my people get me

everything they could on you, but there's one thing I don't know. What makes Ahnd tick? What do you want out of life?"

Areth talked a lot. He was also nosey. Ahnd wasn't sure if he liked that or not, but he also didn't know the answer to the man's questions.

Ahnd shrugged. "Taking chances. Getting better. No plans."

"A man of few words. I can appreciate that. Can't say I'm the same, but I like your take on life. One thing, though. Planning is the way to secure a better future. We don't just get better. We practice and reach our goals to get better. I have a suggestion for you—a potential goal—that you might like. I think it'll be right up your alley. Are you interested?"

"Goals ain't bad."

"Great. First, I have to make sure you're fit for it. I want you to fight Terry over there," he said, pointing to a man who stepped forward.

Built like a transport and a good amount over six-feet-tall, Terry was almost three times bulkier than Ahnd and more than a few inches taller, though Ahnd was growing fast. His hands were big enough to grasp Ahnd's head in just one of them and squeeze it like a pimple. If Ahnd ever saw an unfair fight, this was it.

Ahnd shook his head. "Goal ain't gonna be getting ass kicked."

"Very good, Ahnd. A man who knows his limits. You passed the test. A lot of guys who come in here are so afraid of me that they take up the fight. A lot of guys end up crawling out of here. You've got some smarts on you."

Areth turned in his chair and put his hands on his knees, leaning toward Ahnd.

"I'm going to make you my gang enforcer. Someone gets out of line, you put them in it. You'll take orders directly from me. No one else. What do you think about that?"

"Future comes with something. What you got?"

"Excellent question. You'll get money and girls —I hear you like girls. You'll have clout; that's also known as rep. You'll be my number one in the gangs, and no one will mess with you. Money, girls, and power. What more does a boy want?"

"No killing. I don't kill."

"I don't kill my boys. I take it we have a deal." Ahnd nodded.

"Boys, send Ahnd 10,000 coin to get him started. And, Ahnd, if you need anything, you reach out directly to me. You're under my protection now."

That much money made Ahnd worry. What, exactly, was he going to be enforcing? Maybe he should have asked. He didn't have to wait long to find out. The next day, he got a message about Wester, an eleven-year-old boy in Travis' gang who had stolen a Mæssan device. He was strong and wiry, keeping the teens at bay. Ahnd's mission was to put him in check and make him pay.

Ahnd crossed into Travis' territory unnoticed. He had a rep, but people didn't know him on sight. He made his way through the alleyways, headed toward the park. That's where Travis setup base. Entering the park, he was instantly noticed.

"Thought you were in Larry's," an older teen said, strutting up. "What are you doing here?"

He went to push Ahnd, but Ahnd sidestepped and swept the kid's feet from under him, making him face plant into the fake grass. He scrambled up and turned around with fists raised. "You—"

"Mesixia. Travis?"

The boy lowered his fists. Word had been spread about the enforcer. Stories were about to start.

"Sorry. Follow me."

They walked a short distance across the park to a grimy, buck-toothed guy with a stupid grin leaning on a dirty barrel. He looked like an out-of-place nerd.

"Trav, Mesixia is here," the older teen yelled, and everyone turned to see.

Ahnd was tall and buff. His proportions made him look as vulnerable as he was good looking. Some of the boys puffed up their chests, but they all took a step back.

"Don't look like much. Enforcer? Seems like the big guy grabbed the wrong name," Trav said.

Ahnd kept his cool, but Trav was dedicated to another purpose. He pushed himself off the barrel and strutted to Ahnd, chest bursting at the seams from his arrogance.

"I don't see a punk like you able to enforce anything."

"Wester?"

"Not telling you shit," he said, spitting.

Ahnd kicked him straight in the nuts, bringing him to his knees, then grabbed his hair and jerked it back, staring him directly in the face and spit in the boy's gaping mouth. "Think so?" he said, flipping Travis' head back as he tried to spit out. "Want the punishment?"

Travis stood up, grabbing his crotch with one hand, and wiping his mouth with another. "You're messed up, dude."

"No. Ahnd Mesixia. Ain't forgetting. Wester?"

"He's running," Travis said, his voice less cocky as he pointed across the field.

It figured. He would run. Ahnd Mæssaned a hoverboard, hopped on, then boosted it with Ementhium vapor to go faster. As he approached Wester, he came in on the kid's left and boosted again, shooting past him with an extended arm that clipped him by the neck. Wester tumbled forward, hands first against the cement, and screamed.

"I didn't do it!" he cried.

Ahnd curved around on his hoverboard, hopping off and vaporizing it, and landed directly in front of Wester. He kicked him in the face and sent Wester rolling to the side, then kneeled down, putting his knee on the boy's chest. He reached down and grabbed the boy's hand, forcing it up. The boy started squirming, so Ahnd punched him in the neck. That got his attention.

"Stealing from bros?"

"No, no! It wasn't me."

Ahnd grabbed the kid's middle finger, then

shoved it backwards hard, busting it at the lower knuckle. The kid screamed and rolled on his side, trying to jerk his hand back. He started crying. Ahnd grabbed the kid's hand and held it back as he drove his knee harder into the kid's chest.

"Stealing from bros?" he asked again, pressing the index finger back.

"I'm sorry. I won't do it again."

"Again? Coming back. No fingers. Get me?"

"Yes. Yes. I won't do it again. I'm sorry. I'm so sorry," the boy said, crying profusely.

Ahnd stood up, then kicked the kid in the side.

"Giving back. Today. Ain't seeing it, coming back."

"I will. I'll bring it back. I'm sorry. Please. Please don't break my fingers."

Ahnd spawned a hoverboard and hopped on it, then zoomed off.

Word on the street spread faster than a new girl in town. Mesixia was the last kid you wanted to see and the first one you wanted to avoid.

Cameraman

Ahnd was a great enforcer, and he'd only gotten better over the last two years. That, and a lot taller now that he was fifteen. He kept his strength up and practiced daily so that he stayed on his toes. His name evoked respect and fear.

Pauly was the latest to get punished. He'd peed himself when he saw Ahnd coming for him. That was more common than you'd think. Boys feared the unknown more than pain, and Ahnd's reputation was for vicious pain. Stupid kid had even tried to fight back. That left blood on Ahnd's hands. He was at a fountain washing it off when a girl approached.

"Is that blood? Are you okay?" she asked, running up to him. His knuckles were bloody, but it wasn't his blood.

"Oh," she said, taking a step back. "Is he okay?"

"Yeah. Gonna be. Ain't gonna lie no more," Ahnd said with a snicker, turning to her.

The girl bowed her head and swallowed. "I

better get going," she said.

"Don't gotta. Name's Ahnd. You?"

"Livia. Livia Yasserton, but you can call me Liv. All my friends do."

Livia's black hair ended in curls that complemented the smile on her triangular face and made her brown eyes stand out. Shorter than Ahnd, but not too short, she looked gentle, but smart. She wasn't Ahnd's type, but she was good looking.

"Live around here?"

"Yeah, I go to core just up the street. You?"

Ahnd shook his head. "Don't do school."

"Okay. I'm with you on that, but my mom insists I go to school. Definitely not going to Alexandria, unless one day I get to visit. I'd love to travel the world."

"Myeinth's big."

"Yes, it is, but can you imagine the other great cities of the world? The different vapors lighting up the cities? It's like magic waiting to be unboxed."

Ahnd looked behind him at the broken down park with garbage strewn around and a gang of rowdy kids circling like vultures on prey, then looked at Liv and raised a brow. "Think same everywhere."

"You're not much for words, are you?"

Ahnd peeled up the edge of his Inves top to show his wound. "Got cut. Brain fluid made it work different."

"Oh," Liv said, putting on an affectionate smile. "Well, I have enough words for both of us. It's nice to meet you, Ahnd." She looked at his scarred knuckle.

"So what do you do if you don't go to school?"

"Enforcer. Making kids stay cool."

"That's got to be a tough job, but you look pretty strong. I bet you're good at it."

That earned a little blush from Ahnd.

"Great people do great things. Not a great guy."

"True, and wise. I believe you can be anything you want to be. What do you want to be?"

"Cameraman," Ahnd said without hesitation.

"I didn't see that coming. Why?"

"Got time?"

Liv shrugged. "I can skip class for one day. Sure. What's up?"

Ahnd Mæssaned a motorcycle and had Liv hop on, then they rode home, but he made her wait outside while he went in and fetched his camera. Coming back out, he hopped on the cycle and took her to the nearest park.

"Stand there," he said, pointing toward a tree with Ementhium vapor streaming up the trunk.

"Little left," he said, positioning her so that two streams went up either side of her.

He set the camera to record, then put it in 4D and overlaid a series of filters, drawing out the blush in her cheeks, the softness of her skin, the shine of her eyes, the twinkle of her stance.

He leaned to the left of the camera and flipped his chin up at her. She came over and he held out the camera for her to look inside, then cued the replay.

She made all kinds of impressed sounds while the replay went on.

"Damn, Ahnd. You make me look good. You're really good at this."

Ahnd blushed. "Like it. World without limits. Magic at my fingertips."

She reached out and pushed his hair back from his forehead and smiled. "I think I know just the person you need to meet."

She placed a call, a hologram of a boy with short, brown hair showing up. He smiled a lot and had some nice clothes.

"He's gotta finish class, but he can meet up with us tonight. Are you doing anything?"

Ahnd shrugged. "Depends on trouble."

"Well, if trouble doesn't find you, find me at 4pm."

"Got you," Ahnd said.

"See you later," she said, and walked off.

Ahnd raised the camera and began exploring the world with his favorite filter until he heard a scream. It hadn't even been a minute, and it was Liv screaming. He dropped the camera, spinning around as it fell by his side, hanging from his neck. A couple of older teens had Liv by the arm.

Ahnd shook his head, then strutted up as they pulled her away.

"Hey," he yelled.

The boys looked back and clearly didn't know Ahnd.

"Mesixia. My protection," he said.

"Oh, yeah. How do I know you're him?"

Ahnd shook his head and walked up to the

mouthy kid. The kid stepped forward, leaving his buddy to hold Liv. Ahnd cocked his head to one side, then the other while looking disaffected.

"Easy," Ahnd said.

"Mesixia wouldn't let me do this," the kid said, raising his hand.

Ahnd kicked him straight in the knee, then delivered a solid uppercut to the jaw.

"Didn't," he said, then walked past the kid toward the friend. The friend let go of Liv and ran away.

Liv bolted up to Ahnd and gave him a hug. "Thank you!"

"Say my name. Ain't gonna mess with you," Ahnd said.

Four o'clock rolled in, and Ahnd let his camera fall to his side. Time to meet Liv's friend, so he pulled her up on his wrist pad.

"Where meeting?"

"Hi, Ahnd. We're going to meet at Daisy's. That okay?"

Ahnd shook his head. "Lifted there. Can't go back."

"Oh, well, how about Everson's?"

"Yeah. Works."

"Great. See you soon."

Everson Eatery was a little uppity for Ahnd. Ahnd hadn't showered in a couple of weeks. They might not let him go in. It was worth a shot. Maybe the friend was good.

He hoverboarded over, hopping off and

vaporizing his board just before the door, then swung the door open.

"Excuse me," a guy at the door said, holding up a hand to stop Ahnd. "You can't come in here."

Ahnd shrugged, looking at Liv, and turned to go.

"Wait, Ahnd. Trib, go help him."

A boy Ahnd's height came over as the waiter looked between the two boys, confused. The kid had a little birthmark on his face that kind of looked like a heart, and a huge smile. He was dressed way too fancy for even a place like this. Adding to his ostentation was a parakeet Adori pet with light blue feathers on its head that gave way to white mechanical wings. Was that an Inves 1000? Was this her friend? He'd never hang with someone like Ahnd. Ahnd was a street rat, not an uppity.

"He's with me, Randy. He's fine."

"Sir, I must protest. We have standards at this restaurant. It'll take extra cleaning after he's gone."

"A thousand coin cover it?"

"Well, sir, I believe that would be more than acceptable, but I'll have to check with the manager."

"While you do that, Ahnd is going to come sit with us."

A thousand coin. Dropped just to chat with a street rat. Definitely an uppity. Who was this punk? Ahnd flipped his chin up at the boy and stuck out his dirty hand. "Ahnd."

Without hesitating, the uppity reached out and took Ahnd's hand and shook it firmly. "Trib. Well,

Tribinius, but everyone except my parents calls me Trib. Come on. Let's get something to eat," he said, brandishing a sincere smile.

They walked over to the table and Trib let Ahnd sit first. He scooted around the booth toward Liv and flipped his chin up at her. "Sup?"

"Well, that's not how I wanted you to meet Trib," she said as Trib sat down and scooted next to Ahnd. "But now you know each other. Ahnd doesn't talk a lot, Trib. Want to tell him about yourself?"

Trib spoke a lot, talking about sports in core and his achievements, then went on about how he recently met Liv at core. They ordered food while he was talking and he didn't skip a beat. He was animated, smiling, friendly, and never once did Ahnd catch a look of condescension. He seemed to see Ahnd for Ahnd, just another kid. And he didn't talk about money. For an uppity, that was surprising.

"So, tell me about yourself," Trib said.

"Gang enforcer. Like cameras. Liv said good meeting you."

"Cameras? Like videography? No way. I've been wanting to start a live stream. Are you any good?"

"He's fantastic. Ahnd, show him the video of me."

Ahnd lifted his camera and cued the video, then held it out for Trib to look into, pressing the play button when he was staring into the lens.

"You for hire?" Trib said seriously.

Ahnd shrugged.

"I'll pay you 500 coin per show until the show earns more than that. Then you get thirty percent. That way, you're guaranteed at least 500 coin."

The waiter set the food down on the table, handing Ahnd an extra napkin. Ahnd glared at him, but took a bite of the sandwich. It was fresh, tasteless. He was used to food a little more...old and pungent.

"What you want?"

"Just record the show, edit it, and post it. That's it. If what you did to Liv's video is any sign, you're going to knock their Inveses off."

Ahnd appreciated the compliment, but wasn't sure if this uppity was playing him or not. Only one way to find out.

"Playing me?"

Trib blinked and looked at Liv. She raised her brows as if she didn't know what Ahnd was talking about. Trib studied Ahnd before replying.

"I'm not playing you. That was a business deal."

"Look. Ain't much. Street rat. Bottom barrel. Why thinking me?"

Trib laughed. It was a sincere laugh, not mocking.

"I get it. I'm an uppity. Rich kid with money to throw around like vapor in a tower. You're a scary guy, to be honest. Gang enforcing street rat. Can't really get any scarier than that. But I see a guy just about my age with skills. You love that camera to make videos like that. I see what you're worth, not where you live. I'm just lucky I've got money, but

95

you're lucky you've got skills."

Trib pulled up the sleeve on his Inves, squishing it up on his biceps and pulled off a panel of his arm, exposing the metal structure underneath, then lifted a leg up on the chair and did the same to it. "I don't have arms or legs. I was born a runt. I wasn't supposed to survive. But I'm here. I can play ball, but that doesn't make a living. I don't really have any skills and I don't want my dad's company."

He closed up the openings on his body and straightened his Inves, then looked Ahnd squarely in the eyes. "I don't have much to offer except a heart on my face, but you have skills. I would do anything to be worth as much as you are."

Again, a lot of words.

Ahnd nodded. "Worth in treating your friends. Skills and money ain't shit. People matter. Gonna call you a friend."

Trib reached out to shake on it, but Ahnd shook his head and formed a fist. Trib followed suit, and Ahnd gave him a fist bump.

"Deal."

Ahnd

Trib kept his word, and Ahnd got to do what he loved. The show would start and Ahnd would come to life, capturing Trib in all his glory. Ahnd took Trib's natural charisma and filtered it to perfection. And the show was taking off. Ahnd was still only earning his 500 coin, but Liv showed him the books and explained them. Soon, he would be getting thirty percent and that would be more than 500 coin. Between what he was earning as an enforcer and as Trib's cameraman, he was getting a nice sized stash.

Trib didn't have a problem spending money. Ever. He even rented a place for them to hang out. The streets were no longer home. They had a pad to crash at. Trib had even given Ahnd a room, but most of the time he fell asleep in his recliner reading his visisheet. Liv always looked at him funny when he turned it sideways or upside down, but Ahnd didn't care. The words needed to make sense.

"Ahnd," Liv said, pushing down his visisheet. "I want to talk with you."

That was the one thing. They talked a lot. Usually to each other, which was fine with Ahnd, but they felt some need to include him in their conversations. He usually just grunted, nodded, or shrugged—it seemed to get the point across. He'd learned to speak only when he had something to say, and then to say just what he needed to.

Ahnd flipped his chin up at her.

"You have a lot of money now. Have you thought of getting out of the gang?"

Ahnd shook his head.

"Why? Look around you. It's a different world for you now. You don't need to hurt others to get by; you can do what you love."

She had a point.

"Gangs don't ditch," he said.

"I just think there's more to life."

"Gotta be who you choose," Ahnd said, and Liv lit up.

"Yes, exactly. Who does Ahnd choose to be?"

She let go of the visisheet and he lifted it back up and continued reading, but she had asked a good question. Who did Ahnd want to be? Areth had once asked him about his future and said he needed to have a plan. Maybe he would understand.

Ahnd sighed, shut his visisheet, and hopped out of his chair.

"Where are you going?" Liv asked as he made for the door.

"Make a choice."

Areth was almost across the street from the

Pad, inside the Lucky Lady, so Ahnd marched across the street and up to the second floor, knocking on the door.

"Ahnd, my boy, come in," Areth said.

"Thinking future," Ahnd said, standing in front of Areth's desk as the man leaned back in his chair, feet up on his desk. "Need one. Got one."

"Yes, you do. Right here. You're the best I've ever had."

Ahnd shook his head.

"Cameraman. Getting out."

Areth sat properly in his chair, taking on a stern look. "That doesn't pay much, son. If you leave here, there's no coming back."

Ahnd grunted agreement.

"And there's a price you have to pay first. I need a replacement, and you have to beat both my guards."

Ahnd groaned.

"Tommy Und. He's got skills," Ahnd said, giving his replacement, then spun around and took his fighting stance.

He'd already known he'd have to fight his way out of this, but it would be his last fight. Two guards, both over six feet tall and built like a city tower. They had three weaknesses. The first? Ahnd was agile, but they were muscle bound. Second? Ahnd was better trained. Third? They were fighting Ahnd Mesixia.

The guards rushed him, and he somersaulted forward, rolling between the two of them. He spun around and kicked one in the back of the knee. The guy came down on one knee and cursed while the other guy spun around and reached out, trying to grab Ahnd by his Inves. Ahnd let him, then when he was chin height on the guy, kicked him right in the balls.

The guy laughed. He was wearing a cup. Ahnd groaned, then leaned in and grabbed him by the shirt just as the first guy threw a punch. The punch flew past the back of Ahnd's head, skimming his skull but hitting enough to hurt. Ahnd reached up and poked the guy holding him in the eyes hard. Not enough to blind him, though he could have. The guy dropped him, then Ahnd slid between his legs as he squatted in pain.

"Come here, you shit," the first guy said while the other guy tended his eyes.

Ahnd jumped up on the desk and spun around, delivering a roundhouse to his head. It barely affected the guy, but it gave Ahnd time to flip his foot around and shove it into the man's neck. The guy grabbed his neck and fell to his knees. Ahnd jumped between the two guys and grabbed them by the hair, then jerked hard. Their skulls ferociously cracked into each other's.

Ahnd spun around and looked Areth in the eyes.

"That enough?"

"Yeah. Get out. You're free. I see I made you too dangerous. You'll have a place here if you want to come back. You were always loyal, and I respect that."

Ahnd nodded, then patted the two guys on the back. They swatted him away, one rubbing his eyes, the other his neck. Ahnd turned around with military finesse and walked out a free man.

"Come on," Trib said the next day with his usual excitement. "It's time for the show."

"What are you doing this time?" Liv asked.

Trib winked at her. "Can't stop the Trib."

He darted out the door and Ahnd grabbed his camera, following swiftly behind.

Trib stopped in the middle of the street and spun around. "We're going to start here."

Ahnd nodded and lifted his camera.

"Liv, will you go to the mailroom door and get the code? We're going into the tower. Just wait there when you're done and play sassy coy when we come over."

"What makes you think you can boss me around?" she said. "That kind of sassy coy?"

"Perfect," Trib said with a wink.

"Ahnd, are you ready?"

Ahnd grunted.

"Perfect. On your cue, Ahnd."

Trib posed and smiled, raising his trademark birthmark heart, then waited.

Ahnd focused the camera and selected the right filter. He was the guy behind the camera. The official cameraman. His only job was to make the star of the show shine. Trib was a good guy and it made Ahnd proud to be the guy behind the camera. He held up his fingers. A brief memory flashed through his head. A picture of his family smiling, a dream he had as a kid. He guessed he had that now. He smiled, then counted down.

    Three.

    Two.

    One.

Thank You

Thank you for reading Ahnd. I hope you enjoyed it! This is part of my new series, The Rise of Tribinius Cantus. You can find out more information about this series on my website.

https://sylas.art

Please take a moment and review your read on Amazon or GoodReads—your reviews are an enormous help to authors.

www.amazon.com/dp/B0CRQ6H8VV

goodreads.com/book/show/204965540-ahnd

Newsletter

For freebies and to stay abreast of all my new works, please sign up for my newsletter:

https://sylas.art/signup

More From Sylas Seabrook

Pure Impurity
Now Available

A prophecy divides a world and masks a war between those with the power to create life and those who covet it. We weather the impending destruction of Earth, survive a doomed planet, and ride the tide of a planet's last age while following the conflict to its inevitable conclusion: a battle for harmony that rocks the very foundations of Existence.

A woman so passionately in love with her husband spends thousands of years in search of him. A creature gives up its home in the desperate hope of saving their species. A fascinated scientist discovers what lies beyond our universe. And a son abandoned by his father seeks to return and take his place as rightful heir. Pure Impurity takes you on a journey like no other to discover the greatness in all of us.

https://sylas.art

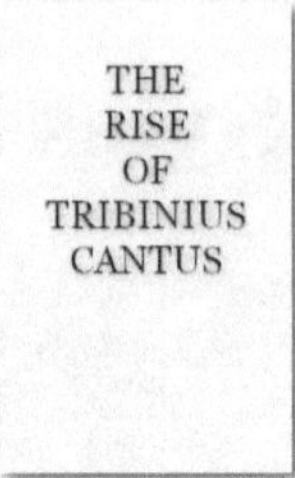

The Rise Of Tribinius Cantus
Coming 2024

A bipolar sixteen-year-old, born without his limbs, stands to inherit one of the largest corporations on Earth, but through his antics, he accidentally helps someone steal the key to his inheritance, a medallion called the Ementhian. He sets out on a quest to recover the Ementhian and in the process discovers a dark secret the corporations are hiding from the world.

https://sylas.art